Rest

LK WOLLETT

Published by LK WOLLETT, 2023.

This is a work of fiction. Similarities to real people, places, or events are entirely coincidental.

REST

First edition. July 16, 2023.

ISBN: 979-8223309741

Written by LK WOLLETT.

Table of Contents

Rest

By LK Wollett

Chapter 1

Parental Discretion Advised

Through the torrent of rain, I saw the car ahead of me careen off the road into the blackness of a field. Both of us were driving too fast perhaps because we both desperately wanted out of this storm. Another car raced by seemingly unaware of what had just occurred. Though I was never inclined to get involved, I slowed down and stopped when I saw the headlights shining toward Heaven. I called 911 with what I saw and the location. Then I ran into the blackness. In seconds, I was soaked and freezing but somehow it didn't matter. The car was overturned; its wheels still spinning. Steam was escaping from the engine. No one was visible on the passenger side so I ran to the driver's side. The sound of sirens was getting closer. The driver's door was open. A woman, a young woman, my age, with blond hair, like mine, was sandwiched between the steering wheel and the back of the seat.

"Help is coming!" I screamed.

She didn't move. I dared not touch her yet I was so scared for her, I wanted to pull her out of there and heal her. A fire truck and squad had turned into the field, heading our direction. Then her head moved toward me; her half-closed eyes focused on me. Her mouth was bloody.

"God is real," she said.

A strong hand touched my arm and gently led me away from the car but my eyes didn't move from the young woman. I wanted her to repeat what she said. I wanted to know what she meant. Why did she say that to me? A fireman put a blanket around my shoulders, held an umbrella over me and walked me to the squad. He was older, like my father, and wanted to know if I needed medical attention. Assuring him I was alright, he put my name and contact information on a form and asked me to sign it. A patrolman, who could have been my brother, joined us wanting to know what happened. I described what I saw. I told him I didn't know the woman when he asked. Another patrolman walked up with a collie on a leash.

"He was in the back seat," the patrolman said. "I thought you might be friends."

"How is she?" I inquired.

The patrolman shook his head.

"She was killed immediately," he replied.

"No!" I blurted. "She spoke to me."

"What did she say?" the patrolman asked with surprise.

"God is real," I answered hesitantly, softly, reverently.

"I don't see how that's possible, Miss," the patrolman declared. "A piece of the steering wheel jammed into her throat. Even if she was alive, I don't see how she could talk."

I stared at the field, wishing for a replay, then looked down and the collie was sitting on my foot.

"He acts like he knows you," the fireman offered. "But I guess you must look like her being her age and with blond hair."

Nodding my head, I was dumbstruck. The collie, in the back seat of the patrolmen's car, stared at me out the back window as it drove away. Focused on the field as though answers were lingering there, I could hear only rain. I eventually realized I was standing in the dark, freezing, with the fireman's blanket and umbrella.

Finally home, so glad to be home, I ran hot water in the tub so I could soak and erase the chill that had settled in my body. Then I planned to finish the leftover chicken in the fridge and call it a day. Thankfully it was Saturday night, meaning no Sunday morning alarm and only chores that I wanted to do like laundry and a little light housekeeping. I also liked making a 'Sunday dinner' that provided leftovers during the week. Most of the time, I stayed in my 'PJ's' which were sweats and a t-shirt with no morning shower or curling iron. Just me in my raw self.

This was my little Shangri-La and I was happy with it. My job, as a computer help-desk manager, Monday through Saturday, required constant people contact which meant constant conversation, both business and social; constant listening; constant compromising; constant persuading; constant defending; constant repeating and sometimes challenging in the most diplomatic way possible. All of it energy-draining. Walking through my own door in my own quiet home at 6 PM was a reward I constantly cherished.

So, why am I not married, a pretty blond in mid-twenties. My theory is that I was an only child of mature parents. I was born, after many years of trying, when they were in their early forties, then apparently, when they gave up trying, I was conceived. Half of my life, they were retired so we traveled the entire country and some foreign countries. Having sown their wild oats, I spent my childhood with two people who were quiet, settled, happy, successful and fun to be with. And they were available. Maybe that is the most important attribute. Therefore, I was always different from my classmates no matter what level of school. Though I tried to socialize and date, the boys to me were rough, silly, and offensive.

The next day, having forgotten or maybe suppressing, the tragic accident, I was loading the washing machine when I heard a dog barking in my front yard. Opening the door just a crack, the collie stopped barking and sat down, looking at me.

"What are you doing here?" I asked wishing he could answer. "You can't stay here."

He had a collar but no tag then it occurred to me that I wanted to return the blanket and umbrella. Leaving the collie on the front porch and sure he wasn't going anywhere, I reluctantly changed clothes and combed my hair. With the blanket and umbrella in hand, I asked the collie if he wanted to go for a ride. He was all for it.

The only fire station I knew was several blocks away. When the collie and I entered what I thought was the front door, there was no receptionist. After a minute, I heard someone in the garage where the firetrucks were parked and I moved in the direction of the voice.

"Excuse me," I said to a fireman walking my way. "I don't know if you can help."

"Yes, Ma'am," said the muscular young man who looked like he was poured into his tee shirt.

"There was an accident in a field last night, about 20 miles north of town," I began. "I was a witness and it was pouring rain. A fireman left his umbrella and blanket with me."

"Thank you, Ma'am," he said taking the items. "I don't know who it was but I can find out."

"One more thing," I added and the young man stopped. "This collie belonged to the young woman who was killed."

The young man looked at the collie with a blank expression then looked at me in the same way. He asked me to wait in the reception area. After waiting impatiently for several minutes, the fireman from the scene of the accident came in and offered his hand.

"So, the collie turned up at your house?" the fireman began as I shook his hand. "I called the family and they confirmed he went missing."

"Can you return him?" I hoped.

"Oh, yes," he responded quickly. "They are glad he was found."

With relief, I thanked him and left, happy to return to my solitude, that was sadly dwindling rapidly.

Monday. If that name does not send even the tiniest hint of sadness throughout your being, you are most fortunate. Sunday and Monday are as different as peace and war; feast and famine; wealth and poverty. It starts with being awakened before you want to get up and then being thrust into a gauntlet of required tasks: shower, curl, dress, drive, start the computer and answer the first phone call from a person who can't get their computer started. Then the remainder of the day will be comprised of similar sentences repeated by a hundred other people.

For that reason, we can skip talking about the day and jump to 6 PM. I pulled into my drive and the collie was sitting patiently on my front porch. Calling the fire department, I, again, had to explain who I was to someone who wasn't aware of the situation and again, thankfully, the fireman who was at the scene got on the phone. Like me, he was amazed at the collie's behavior and said he would contact the family.

I pulled leftovers out of the fridge and filled a plate. Just as I sat down, there was a knock on the door. When I opened it, a couple, was looking at me. They had the collie on a leash.

"Hello," said the woman with a warm smile.

She was one of those petite ladies who aged beautifully. Her handsome, well-groomed husband stood close to her as though ready to protect her if needed.

Reluctantly, I opened the door and invited all of them in, including the collie.

"I'm Margaret and this is my husband, Jeff," the lady offered.

Jeff nodded with a smile.

"I'm Jane," I responded, smiling, wishing they would leave.

"I'm sorry Ty has been bothering you," Margaret stated.

"It's alright, really," I lied, thinking about my plate of food.

"He misses Jill so much," Margaret explained with sadness.

Ty, on cue, let out a little cry and seemed to nod in agreement. Sadness overtook me also now that I was focused on their pain rather than my plate.

"I'm so sorry about, your daughter?" I consoled.

"Yes, our daughter, Jill," Margaret answered. "Your age I imagine. Now that I see you, I can see why Ty is attracted to you. You could have been sisters."

The pain in Margaret's voice was becoming noticeable.

"We need to go, Dear," Jeff said softly.

Margaret walked toward the door.

"Thank you, Jane," Jeff offered.

Again, my solitude disrupted, I was irritated as I ate my leftovers and put my plate in the dishwasher. Knowing the morning alarm would attack me in a few hours, I tried to relax and sleep. However, the recurring visit of the collie and seeing the pain in the parents made me remember what Jill had said, "God is real." Had anyone at anytime said that to me, I would have given it no thought because I agreed with them. I never knew anyone who said he wasn't real. Of course, there are atheists, but I never met one and, I would have let them believe what they want. I'm not their boss; I can't make them believe anything. When Jill said, "God is real," it had a substance that I never experienced. It had weight. Even though the sentence was comprised of familiar words, they came out different when she said them.

Eventually, I fell asleep and woke the next day to my normal routine including the collie sitting on my porch at 6 PM. This time, however, as soon as I pulled out my phone to call the fire department, someone knocked on the door. Jeff was there.

"Hi," I said, laughing.

"Hello," he replied, also laughing, as he put the leash on the collie.

"We have to stop meeting like this," I joked. I was using my computer manager happy-face facade as though talking to the person who can never get their computer started.

Jeff chuckled.

"Don't tell Margaret," he whispered, still chuckling as he led the collie to his car.

Chapter 2

The third appearance of the collie on my doorstep was the last, to my knowledge, anyway. I was happily looking forward to my comfortable routine when a police officer appeared at my door with a few questions about the accident. Looking at a report, she asked me to confirm some details like the time, location and what I actually saw. I relayed that, after the car swerved into the field, I had run to it and saw the young woman sandwiched between the steering wheel and the back of the seat.

"Did you touch her or anything?" the officer asked.

"No," I replied, wondering if I had left-over green beans.

"Did you see the dog?"

"No."

"Did you see her phone?"

"No."

"Can you recall anything, anything that you haven't reported?" the officer pressed. "Any animals on the road? Was the road flooded? Any other cars..."

"Yes!" I blurted, suddenly remembering. "Another car did pass and it was speeding. But it didn't stop."

"Did its break lights come on?" the officer asked.

"I don't know. I wasn't watching it," I responded trying to relive the moment. "I followed the woman's car for several miles. Both of us were speeding."

An involuntary laugh escaped as I realized I had indicted myself; I looked down with embarrassment. The officer waited patiently, not revealing what she was thinking.

"I never saw that car behind me," I finally finished.

"But it was dark and raining hard, correct?" the officer suggested.

"That's true," I agreed. "It could have been there without my knowledge."

This was starting to sound sinister and I wanted badly to ask if something was wrong yet, like I mentioned, I tend not to get involved.

The next day, my phone rang with an unfamiliar number and I let it go into voice mail.

"Hi, this is Bailey Cardell. I'm a lawyer investigating the accident of Jill Hilledebrand. I'd like to meet with you. Perhaps we can meet for lunch? Please call me."

Wanting no part of Miss Cardell, I assumed the only escape was to get it over with so I called her number and arranged to meet for lunch on Saturday. Then I requested a half day of vacation on Saturday afternoon. I was needing to recharge after spending energy on these unwanted interruptions.

On Saturday, I found the restaurant using GPS, the greatest invention ever! When I pulled in, a middle-aged woman, in a light brown jacket and matching skirt, was waiting at the front door and she waved at me. I stopped to speak to her. Confirming she was Bailey Cardell, I parked and walked to her. She walked so briskly toward a table, I rushed to keep up then she pulled out a chair for me and pointed at a waiter.

"My guest is here," she announced for the entire restaurant to hear.

Eating out was unusual for me since my parents' deaths. As a family that traveled often, we ate at restaurants often. Since then, though, I preferred to choose my own food and prepare it myself.

"So, Jane," Bailey began, "tell me about the accident."

I repeated everything I had told the officer which Bailey seemed to accept with no issues.

"Have you been in contact with the Hilledebrands?" Bailey asked.

I didn't like this question and wondered if I should be talking to Bailey.

"Indirectly," I replied, cautiously.

This answer puzzled Bailey and she folded her hands under her chin to reveal perfectly polished nails, a couple of gold rings, one of them with a stunning diamond, and gold bracelets falling away from her hands. I admired that she took time to apply makeup, something I never cared for.

"Indirectly?" she repeated. "How could you interact with them indirectly?"

I told her about the collie showing up on my doorstep and that Margaret and Jeff retrieved it once then Jeff retrieved it a second time.

"Oh, how interesting," Bailey responded as the food arrived. "You never met Jill or the dog or her fiancé?"

"No, never," I affirmed. "I'm not a social person. I work, eat, sleep then work, eat, sleep..."

Laughing at myself, Bailey politely laughed with me.

"How could the collie know where you live?" Bailey wondered.

"There's no way he could know," I replied firmly and I didn't mind showing some irritation.

She needed to understand clearly that I was certain about what I was saying.

"I'm not connected to them in any way. I'm not connected to anyone, Miss Cardell," I insisted.

Unexplainably, that last sentence seemed to echo: "I'm not connected to anyone...anyone...anyone."

Having paid the bill, Bailey walked briskly to the door then stopped on the sidewalk, thanked me for meeting her and offered her card. With no intention of ever calling her, I took the card.

Planning to enjoy my afternoon off by going to the mall then grocery shop, I was devastated when a messenger knocked on my door. He handed me an envelope from the County Courthouse - a subpoena. I needed to testify at a hearing regarding the accident.

"How could this be happening to me?" I cried to myself. "Why did I choose to get involved this time?"

On Monday at work, because I was going to need a day off for the hearing, I told my supervisor, Allison, about the subpoena which led to my telling her the entire story. Normally, our conversations centered around someone's computer or their inability to use it so sharing this much private information was unusual. I knew little about her personal life aside from a few pictures in her office of her husband, I assumed, and her children, all boys, I assumed. She did ask me about my personal life when we first met but she soon wisely realized that my life was simple, uninteresting and I didn't want to share.

On subpoena day, I gave myself enough time to get lost, which I did a lot, and so I was at the courthouse early. At the room stated on the subpoena, an officer checked me in and I sat in the back row. As the hearing time approached, Margaret and Jeff arrived and found a seat at the front of the room, same side as me. Jeff had his arm on the back of the seat as though cradling Margaret. Bailey came in next and sat in the same row but on the opposite side of the aisle. She looked at them and they looked back. A tall, slender man, my age, sandy brown hair, in a dark navy suit came in, stopped next to my row, looked around then headed toward Margaret and Jeff. The bailiff introduced the judge and read the names involved in the case. One of the names was Jill Hilledebrand and the other was Dennis Cliff.

After testimony was heard by the two patrolmen and the fireman, my name was called. I rose with dread and walked toward the judge. The bailiff led me to the witness stand and I was sworn in. When he stepped aside, I saw Dennis Cliff, on the left side of the room seated at a table with Bailey. He was a tall, slender man, my age, with sandy brown hair in a gray suit. My eyes moved to the right side of the room and his twin, name unknown, the tall man in the dark navy suit, was seated with Margaret and Jeff.

A lawyer I assumed, sitting in front of Margaret and Jeff, walked to me, asked me, in one of those deep, deep voices, my name, age, where I worked, where I lived, if I lived with anyone. He asked me to relay what I saw the night of the accident. I obliged and he sat down.

Bailey walked to me and asked me, as she did in the restaurant, if I knew Margaret and Jeff. I repeated, as I did in the restaurant, that I did not know them.

"How did the collie know where you live, Miss Fortner?" Bailey questioned.

A fire burst in my stomach wanting to incinerate this woman.

"As I told you in the restaurant," I announced to the onlookers, "I have no idea. I never met any of these people."

"It makes no sense to me that a collie you never saw before would travel over 20 miles to a house he had never been to," Bailey pressed, looking at the jury.

"I guess you have to ask the collie, Ma'am," I retorted.

The lawyer sitting in front of Margaret and Jeff stood and asked if he could approach the bench. It seems I was correct to mention the restaurant because this was a violation of some kind; apparently Bailey was supposed to share this conversation with the prosecution before bringing it before the jury. The judge said the hearing was suspended pending further notice and the bailiff told me I was free to go. The tall man in the navy suit was watching me walk away from the witness stand. As I moved passed the lawyer who was sitting in front of Margaret and Jeff, he said my name; I stopped.

"I'm David Stone, representing Jill Hilledebrand," he stated. "Do you have a lawyer?"

He may as well have punched me in the stomach.

"No," was all I could muster. "Why?"

He pulled out a card.

"You need a lawyer," he advised and turned away.

With a sigh, I took a step toward the exit, avoiding eye contact with Margaret and Jeff.

"What is happening?" I cried to no one.

I got home at 6 PM, usually my happy time. Today, I needed to call this stranger so I called him.

"Bartholomew Thomas," I read to myself from the card. "Who names their child Bartholomew?"

The phone rang.

"Hello, BT speaking," said the youthful voice.

"This is Jane Fortner," I began but didn't need to finish.

"Yes, David told me you would be calling. When can we meet?" he asked.

I took a deep breath, wanting to exhale my frustration.

"Wait a minute. Meet about what?" I exclaimed. "I have no idea what is going on."

"We can meet and I'll explain," BT offered.

"No!" I cried. "I don't know any of you people! This is a nightmare!"

"Okay, okay," BT replied softly. "Listen to me."

"Okay," I replied letting my irritation show and I sat in my favorite chair, keenly aware that I had not yet eaten.

BT began: "Jill Hilledebrand was killed in the wreck you witnessed. As she was driving, she was on her phone to her parents. She said she was racing home to get away from Dennis Cliff, the man you saw in the courtroom today."

"Were you there today?" I interrupted.

"I was there," he answered, then continued. "Jill had been complaining for months that Dennis was stalking her but it could never be proven. That night, she managed to record an episode of his attempt to rape her."

"Oh!" escaped from my lips. "How horrible!"

"Somehow," BT continued, "only God knows how, she got away from him with the recording. So now, Dennis has been charged with manslaughter and the lawyer, Bailey, is desperate to win the case."

"Only manslaughter?" I questioned. "What about attempted rape?"

BT sighed.

"The phone is missing," he replied. "There is no evidence to support attempted rape."

"How could the phone be missing?" I wailed. "No-one came near the car!"

"Did the car turn over in the field?" BT challenged softly.

He was making me realize that the phone could be anywhere in the field.

"Weren't you the only person in contact with her before she died?" he continued.

"For a few minutes!" I cried. "In pouring rain!"

"With the right words to the right people, Bailey can make you a suspect," BT concluded.

"Suspect of what?" I stammered in disbelief.

"You are in love with Dennis and you were in pursuit of Jill wanting to retrieve the phone," BT theorized.

I was outraged and nearing hysteria.

"NO WAY!" I screamed. "No way that can be proven!"

"Listen," BT began, "think about it. Pray about it. Call me if I can help. Or don't call. It's your decision."

His voice had a soothing, calming effect.

"Okay," I replied, ending the call.

In my kitchen, I stared at my leftovers. Nothing looked good. In the back of the fridge was a bottle of wine which had been there for ages. I pulled it out and poured a glass. It was 9 PM, only one hour left to my bed time. I filled the glass again. Then tears burst through a barrier I had erected years ago after my father died; I cried myself to sleep.

Chapter 3

When the alarm went off, I didn't want to move, but, my adult self rose and began the morning routine. When I arrived at my desk, my computer was gone. My body froze; my brain froze. My supervisor, Allison, came in.

"Jane," she said, "your computer was confiscated by police this morning."

My lips formed the word, "what?" but no sound came out. Allison touched my arm then turned toward her office. I followed.

"I'm so glad you shared that accident with me," Allison began. "If I hadn't known those details..."

I nodded knowing what she was going to say.

"We have to go to Personnel," Allison stated and she rose.

The personnel manager, while sympathetic and understanding, explained that what happened was disruptive and it would be best if I took leave of absence. My brain was numb so I just agreed with whatever he said. Allison asked me if I needed anything from my office and I didn't. She hugged me and gave me her card.

"Call me anytime," she said. "We can get through this."

Tears welled in my eyes and she held me as I sobbed. When I calmed down, she escorted me to the exit.

"Jane," she repeated as we parted. "Call me anytime."

In my car, I called BT.

"They took my computer at work," I declared with tears escaping again.

"Where are you?" he asked with urgency.

I told him I was in a parking garage.

"Stay there! I'm coming to you!" he practically shouted.

In ten minutes or so, my phone rang.

"I'm at the garage! What level? What kind of car?" BT exclaimed.

I gave him the level number and described my car. A family van shortly stopped behind me and a short young man with black curly hair jumped out. He was wearing a red checkered shirt over a black tee shirt and jeans. I opened the window.

"BT," he greeted, smiling, offering his hand.

I looked up at him and shook his hand.

"Jane," I replied.

"Where can we talk?" he asked.

"Can you see the coffee shop across the street?" I offered.

He nodded that he did and we walked there. I ordered coffee and a cookie; he ordered coffee. He let me pay and we found a seat near the window.

"If they took your computer, they will want your phone," BT stated immediately. "They will search your home."

At this point, I was catatonic.

"Whatever," I stated, rolling my eyes.

"Is your phone backed up?" BT asked.

I pulled it out and started the backup process.

"It is now," I replied.

"You've heard of planting evidence, haven't you?" BT suggested.

Scoffing and shaking my head, I put my hand to my forehead and started to laugh.

"This is one bad movie," I declared. "It looks like you got the job. Where do I send your retainer? I better send it now before they close my bank account."

Thankful that I had accumulated extra funds for a vacation, I sent him the money. Stopping at an ATM on my way back to the car, I got cash in the event they did close my bank account. I wasn't going to be surprised at anything at this point. He followed me home and the police were there. Four squad cars with lights blazing. Neighbors were standing on their lawns. An officer handed me an envelope which I gave to BT and introduced him as my lawyer. I let them all in.

As they rummaged through drawers and closets, lifting cushions off the couch and removing bed clothes, the room closed in on me. It's like my brain was shutting down.

"God is real," echoed in the blackness. "Pray about it."

When my eyes opened, I was in a hospital room with a tube in my mouth and in my arm. I had to use the bathroom. I knew, from visiting my mother in the hospital, that a nurse button was somewhere. Finding a remote with a red button, I pushed it. In moments, a nurse entered.

"Jane!" she exclaimed with an open mouth grin. "Jane, you're back!"

I nodded. She leaned down.

"I need to get some help," she said. "I'll be back in a few minutes."

Looking around the room, cards and drawings made by children were taped everywhere. A short man came in and introduced himself but I didn't catch his name. He explained that I had been unconscious for three days and he had to remove some tubes. He did so with as much gentleness as possible but it made my chest burn. I nodded 'yes', that I was in pain when he asked. He told the nurse what to give me.

"I have to use the bathroom," I tried to say but my voice was weak and my throat hurt.

The nurse helped me walk to the bathroom. Normally I would have balked at having anyone in the bathroom with me, but I was totally surrendered to this nightmare that had become my life.

"I'm Anna," she said. "Do you want to shower?"

"I don't think I can right now," I answered.

"Hello?" said a voice. It was BT's voice.

"One moment, please," Anna responded.

Looking in the mirror as I washed my hands, a deep sigh escaped as I saw my oily, uncombed hair and felt my gaunt, pale face.

"Did I lose weight?" I whispered.

Anna helped me into bed and got me covered.

"I can order tomato soup, if you like," she offered.

"That sounds good, thank you," I replied with genuine gratitude.

"Applesauce? Milk?" she suggested.

I nodded with a smile like I used to do with my mother. Anna left and she let BT in.

"Hi there," he said impishly.

Pushing a button to raise the top of the bed, I waved at him. My body didn't have the strength to sit up.

"You sure know how to scare a guy," BT stated.

I chuckled.

"I've been told that before," I quipped then brushed my hair back. "I looked really scary in the mirror just now."

We laughed.

"Thank you for coming," I said.

"Of course," he responded. "I'm glad you're awake. So scary, Jane."

He pulled up a chair.

"What did the doctor say?" he started. "If I may ask. You don't have to share."

"I literally *just* woke up," I replied. "I haven't heard anything."

BT nodded.

"So I guess I fainted," I suggested.

"Yes, you fainted. An officer sat you on a chair and put your head between your knees. I guess that works sometimes."

BT smiled after that statement.

"You weren't waking up so they called the squad and...you just kept sleeping," he continued.

I sighed.

"I'm your next of kin, by the way," he smiled, "if anyone asks."

"Oh," I responded, knowing immediately what he was referring to. "I didn't have anyone designated, did I?"

"Well, you do, at work," he answered.

"At work?" I interrupted.

"Yes, I called Allison to get your next of kin," he explained. "A number was listed but it was disconnected."

I laughed at myself.

"I don't remember who I wrote down," I admitted. "I probably made it up."

"Thankfully, the hospital let me sign papers to get you a room," BT recounted. "Allison is aware and will confirm my legitimacy if needed."

A technician came to take readings and the food tray arrived.

"Getting crowded in here," BT observed. "I'll take off and catch you tomorrow, alright?"

He held out his hand and I took it with both of mine.

"Thank you," I said sincerely. "I appreciate you taking time for me."

"Happy to do so," he replied with a warm smile and a warm glow in his eyes.

I knew he meant it.

The next morning, a different nurse, Theresa, woke me to order breakfast and she helped me shower. With a clean hospital gown, clean sheets and clean blanket, I felt quite refreshed. A doctor came in. My father's age had he lived, I guessed; a little taller though.

"Jane Fortner?" he asked. "I'm Michael Strand."

Then he pointed to his badge.

"MD," he stated laughing.

He made me laugh. He was looking at a computer tablet. I was wondering when breakfast would arrive.

"So you slept for three days," he relayed, "and we can't determine the reason at this time. You were dehydrated. Are you dieting or fasting?"

A deep sigh escaped.

"No," I replied shaking my head. "I was dealing with a stressful situation, and I wasn't hungry."

"So that would affect your blood sugar count and your blood pressure," he declared as he pounded on the tablet. "Your vital signs are good now so I see no reason to keep you. What do you think?"

"I think that's great," I agreed.

"We'll call, ah," he paused and looked at the tablet, "Bartholomew?"

"Yes," I nodded and laughed. "Bartholomew."

He patted the bed then left. I could smell coffee from the hall and saw the cart of breakfast trays approaching. So far, it was a good morning.

After breakfast, a technician came in to get readings and, shortly after, Theresa arrived stating that I could get dressed to leave. She pointed to some drawers beside the bed and I found my belongings.

"Hello?" BT said from the other side of the door.

"Hold on," I replied. "I'm getting dressed."

Not wanting to keep him waiting, I rushed and glanced in the mirror. My hair was straight and flat but not oily, at least.

"Come in," I said.

BT walked in with a little girl at his side.

"Hi there," he greeted and smiled impishly and patted the girl's head. "This is Pumpkin."

"Nooo, not Pumpkin," the little girl protested, giggling, as she lightly smacked his arm. "Patty."

She looked at me still giggling. I extended my hand to her and she shook it.

"This is Jane," BT added.

"Is this your dad?" I asked Patty.

She nodded her head and wrapped her arms around his waist, hugging him tightly. He put his hand on her back and patted it. It was quite surprising to me that BT could have a daughter this age.

"How old are you?" I inquired.

"I'll be eight years old on Saturday," she announced happily.

I looked seriously at BT.

"You don't look old enough," I declared.

"Yeah," he agreed shaking his head. "I'm older than I look."

Another nurse entered the room with a wheel chair.

"Ready to go?" she asked me. "Got everything?"

That made me want to look so I opened drawers.

"What about the pictures?" Patty exclaimed and she pointed at one. "That one is mine."

"Oh, wow!" I fretted. "How could I forget them? Who made all these?"

"Patty asked her friends at church to make them," BT explained.

Then I looked directly at her.

"Thank you so much," I said, then I pandered like she was one of my computer associates. "They helped me get well."

BT and I pulled down the pictures and cards and handed them to Patty. She lovingly put them away in a bag I provided. In BT's van, we talked about Patty's school and her upcoming birthday party. Another younger brother was at home, Matthew, four years old, and BT's wife, Ruth, was pregnant. After a few miles, I realized that BT was taking me home and the walls started to close in on me again.

"BT!" I cried. "I can't go back there!"

He said nothing then he studied me at a red light.

"Do you have any relatives?" he asked.

"I never met any," I replied. "We never visited relatives. My parents didn't talk about family, at all."

"High school friends, college? Church?" he pressed as the light turned green. "Bingo?"

"No," I stated with a chuckle. "Just my mother and father."

"I don't remember meeting anyone as isolated as you," BT mused. "You're like an orphan."

I didn't care to respond. My life was fine until the accident. I opened my purse and was happy to see my phone.

"The police didn't take my phone?" I marveled.

"They talked about it but, since you were asleep, they couldn't get into it," BT explained.

"One good outcome in this chaos," I smiled.

I looked at my bank account and it had money. I looked for the cash I had withdrawn and it was where I put it.

"Would you take me to the Gladstone Hotel?" I requested.

"The Gladstone? Whoo-Hoo!" BT teased. "You go for the best."

"Yes, Sir," I nodded. "I like my comfort."

"And security," I thought to myself. "The best security is a 'must' at these five-star hotels."

He stopped at the entrance of the hotel.

"Can I call you tomorrow about the case?" BT asked.

I reluctantly nodded, thanked him, and turned to Patty to say 'good-bye' and 'thank you'. She handed me the pictures and cards. When they pulled away, I focused on the luxurious accommodations ahead of me, ready to escape from reality.

Chapter 4

It was embarrassing to check in with no luggage but I quickly explained that the airport was looking for it. I headed for the shops and bought a tooth brush, floss and other toiletries. Then I was able to find a few outfits at reasonable prices plus comfortable shoes, undergarments, sweats, slippers and a couple of trendy t-shirts. The help in these luxurious shops are so wonderful and a porter, who hung my clothes on a mobile rack, followed me to my room. It was my pleasure to tip him generously.

Next, I was able to get into the salon for a hair cut and massage. My mother lived to look good for and take care of her husband. He was a charmer. I mean, he knew how to make you feel like you were the only person in his life. While she seemed to love every minute with me, she came alive when he appeared. Likewise, when he entered a room, his first action was to make contact with her. There were rumors that he had affairs, but, if they were true, he hid them well. Having been labeled an orphan by BT, I saw now that she also was an orphan. Both of them were, it seemed.

Completely relaxed after a few hours in the salon, I called Allison, although my motives were selfish. I wanted her help getting my job back and wondered if all those boys could help me move.

"Jane," Allison cried. "Thank you for calling. I was so worried after BT asked for your..."

"Thank you for letting me call," I replied, cutting her off. "I'm all better now."

She wanted to know everything but I deflected.

"Is my computer returned?" I asked.

"It isn't," she stated with irritation. "It will be gone as long as that case is open, I'm afraid."

"That's true," I agreed. "Is there any chance I can come back?"

"I checked with them today and they want to wait for the case to be closed," she relayed.

I sighed. A man's voice was talking to Allison but I couldn't hear their words.

"Sorry," Allison chuckled. "Alex is making supper. Do you want to come to supper?"

Normally, I would have made up a reason not to go but, this time, I agreed.

"Alright," I said. "What's your address?"

The concierge got me a cab and I realized Allison lived in the same area as the accident. Though I didn't want to, I stared at the upcoming spot and a car was parked there. A man was sitting in the driver seat.

"Was that one of the twins?" I asked myself, wishing I could stop the cab to find out for sure.

Allison's house was surrounded by several acres of manicured lawn that could have been mistaken for a golf course. At the end of the very long driveway was a pickup, a nice van and a few other cars. As I walked toward the door, Allison opened the screen and greeted me.

"You found us!" she declared.

When I got within arms' length of her, she hugged me. A bald man, my height, with a protruding belly, walked to the door.

"Alex," Allison began. "This is Jane Fortner."

He extended his hand and I shook it.

"You're in for a treat!" he exclaimed. "My special recipe chili with homemade bread."

"He got a bread maker," Allison explained.

"Sounds good to me," I responded smiling and hoping the chili would be as good as he claimed.

Allison led me to the dining room. Her decor was 'country' I guess with warm colors, ruffled curtains and cushions on the Early American-style couch. A large brown dog lay by the fireplace, thankfully oblivious to me. Alex was filling bowls of chili as Allison tossed salad.

"Anything I can do?" I offered.

"Have a seat," Allison replied and put salad in front of me. "What kind of dressing?"

"I like most of them," I replied. "Italian, Ranch..."

Allison set one of each on the table.

"Supper's ready!" Alex bellowed.

Doors opened down the hall and the air filled with the raucous laughter and yelling of teenage boys.

"Boys!" Allison scolded. "We have a guest."

Immediate silence followed as the three teenage boys took their seats. Allison sounded off their names and ages and they all politely nodded. Alex gave them bowls of chili and Allison passed the bread, salad and dressing. Then, as though practiced, they bowed their heads to give thanks.

The supper conversation centered around the boys, their place in school, sports and college. As each boy finished their food, they rinsed their plates and put them in the dishwasher. It was impressive. As the sun was setting, I mentioned that I should call a cab and Allison, thankfully, offered to take me to the hotel.

"You have to be proud of your sons," I stated as we drove down the long driveway.

"I praise God for them every day," Allison responded, "and my husband, my home, my blessed life."

"I never knew you were religious," I observed.

"That's good," Allison replied to my surprise. "I'm not religious."

"But you just said...", I began.

"I follow Jesus," Allison explained. "Jesus wasn't religious either."

We were approaching the location of the accident.

"The accident happened here," I announced, interrupting her.

Allison looked toward the field.

"A car was parked there earlier," I added. "It looked like one of the men from the courtroom was sitting in the driver seat."

"Mourning, perhaps?" Allison wondered.

Picturing Dennis in the gray suit sitting beside Bailey in the courtroom and his twin, Name Unknown, sitting beside Margaret and Jeff, I nodded in agreement.

"Perhaps," I agreed. "One of them tried to rape her; maybe the other one loved her."

"Oh," Allison uttered softly, "sounds like one of those hot romance novels."

We laughed and I decided I could share what Jill said.

"She spoke to me," I relayed softly.

Allison waited.

"She said 'God is real,'" I continued.

"That's quite a statement from a dying person," Allison declared. "I'd love to know her relationship with God."

I thought of my mother in a hospital bed, weak, thin, barely able to speak. I remembered her closing her eyes never to open them again and my father sobbing. Tears wet my face.

"I'm sorry, Jane," Allison offered gently as she touched my arm. "That was a thoughtless remark."

"No, no," I sighed and used my shirt to wipe my face. "This whole horrible situation has brought up memories of my parents."

"I'm sorry," Allison repeated.

Allison pulled up to the hotel and asked me to keep in touch. I said I would, but I really didn't want to involve her any more. Meeting her family made me realize that they could become suspects. So I decided to make a call I didn't want to make. It was a call of desperation.

Before going to my room, I bought a prepaid phone. Assuming my every action was being monitored now, I wanted to call a number I hadn't called since my parents' deaths.

"Hello," said the man's voice that was weaker than I remembered.

"Ronald," I responded.

"Jane?" he replied.

"Yes," I answered.

"Hold on," he said.

I heard rustling and muffled voices.

"Jane, what's wrong?" he asked.

"I think I'm being tracked," I stated.

Ronald was silent for a minute.

"I've got this number you're calling from," he began. "In 30 minutes, I'll call back."

On the luxurious couch, I flipped through the TV channels landing on an orchestra playing something classical; Bach maybe. Speaking to Ronald made me go back to the day he called that my father had died of a heart attack. Not only had he died but he was already buried. Ronald said my father insisted that I stay at college and not be notified of the funeral. It was then Ronald revealed my father's wealth and my father's fear that the money would put me in danger. For that reason, Ronald managed the estate and told me how to contact him when needed.

The prepaid phone rang.

"Jane," Ronald stated urgently. "What's wrong!"

I repeated all the details.

"So you need money," Ronald concluded immediately then continued. "We need to get the house sold, utilities cut off and your belongings moved..."

"Wait," I interrupted. "Would you get rid of that stuff? I'll buy new stuff."

Ronald didn't respond.

"Please, Ronald?" I begged.

"Such a waste..." Ronald replied.

"You know people who can use it, don't you?" I suggested.

"Everything?" Ronald asked. "There's nothing...?"

"Everything of value to me was taken long ago," I responded with tears again flowing. "You know that."

A deep sigh came through the phone.

"Yes, I do know that," Ronald agreed. "Anything else?"

"I hope that's all," I tried to joke.

Ronald paused and I heard muffled voices.

"A messenger will bring a laptop," Ronald began. "On it will be a link to a checking account with funds along with passwords and a debit card. I'll include another prepaid phone. Call me when you get the laptop."

When he hung up, I discarded the phone after I had disabled it, something my father taught me to do, then I dressed for bed. As I searched for houses on my phone, I realized I needed a car and also realized I didn't mention the car to Ronald. No way I was calling him back for that; tonight's conversation was a risk that could bring a lot of problems into his life. His situation was actually like mine: an innocent person being harassed.

My phone rang and it was BT. He wanted to meet tomorrow which was fine. We decided on a time and I mentioned that I needed to get my car. The next morning, I was waiting at the door of the hotel when BT pulled up. We drove to my house and it had a 'for sale' sign.

"You're selling the house?" BT exclaimed.

"Yes," I answered offering no explanation.

It didn't surprise me that curtains were already taken down. Had I cared to look in the house, I'm sure it would have been empty. Fully intending to open the garage door and retrieve my car, I started to get out of BT's van when a car pulled up to the curb of my house.

"A car just pulled up," I stated.

BT turned around to look.

"A light blue, older car," he described. "A classic car, I'd say. One of those gas-guzzlers."

I didn't look.

"Can you see the driver?" I asked whispering though not sure why.

"It's a man," BT began. "I can't see his head. It could be Dennis."

"If it's Dennis, I can't get my car now," I stated. "He can't know where I'm staying."

BT pulled away.

"Try to see who it is," I urged.

"He's too tall," BT exclaimed. "Let's circle back and watch him."

At the next cross roads, BT turned left then left again then left again. We turned onto my street about three blocks from my house; BT parked. The blue gas-guzzler was sitting there.

"Take some pictures," BT suggested. "Try to get his license number."

"What is he doing here, anyway?" I asked myself mostly, knowing BT wouldn't have an answer.

"He shouldn't be here, for sure," BT declared. "Everyone knows not to contact you. It would strengthen Bailey's case."

"Indeed," I affirmed. "So we might conclude that this is Dennis and he is also trying to strengthen Bailey's case."

Adjusting my phone to magnify the picture, I got a picture of his license then he got out of the car and walked toward the house. He looked in the window of the house then looked in the garage.

"I'd love to be there when Bailey hears that you moved!" BT laughed.

"Now he knows my car!" I wailed. "I can't drive that car!"

We watched the man drive off.

"Drive your car to my house," BT suggested.

I nodded in agreement and stated that I wanted to sell the car.

When we arrived at BT's house, an old two story with attic, in an old neighborhood with small front lawns and large back yards, he introduced me to his wife, Ruth, huge with child, who was vacuuming; the children were in the back yard. BT led me to his office where we listed my car for sale. Then we talked about the case.

"The next hearing is in two weeks," BT started. "You will again be asked to testify and you will again have to refute Bailey's accusations. She may ask why you moved. The family will all testify that they don't know you. They will have to explain why they went to your house two times. Dennis is listed as a witness for himself but Bailey could choose not to call him."

"What if the jury gets confused?" I wondered.

"He might be declared 'not guilty,'" BT answered.

"I should never have left my car that night," I sighed, looking to Heaven.

"Things happen for a reason," BT offered.

He let me study him for a few seconds. All his attention was on me and his eyes were full of concern.

"She spoke to me," I relayed. "She said, 'God is real.'"

"Wow," he responded softly. "That's quite a statement for someone who is dying."

"That's what Allison said," I replied with an involuntary laugh.

"I'm taking that as a message for you," BT began, "from God, himself. I'd advise that you take it seriously."

"What do you mean?" I wondered, having no idea what he meant.

"I mean, all of us would live our lives so differently if we KNEW that God was real," BT stated. "If we KNEW we would meet him someday and try to explain our lives."

"What's wrong with my life?" I retorted with irritation. "I rarely drink or smoke, I don't steal or lie..."

"That's all good," BT interrupted, "but God wants more than good behavior. He wants your attention. He wants you to know him; to love him."

"How can I know him?" I challenged. "I can't see him or hear him."

"We know him by reading the Bible and talking to him, praying to him," BT explained.

As though BT thought that was enough Bible lesson for today, he suggested that he take me back to the hotel. As we walked past Ruth, she shut off the vacuum and BT stood close to her as she spoke to him; she looked up at him like he was everything in her life.

At the hotel I was relieved that Ronald's laptop had arrived. In my room, I connected to a private vpn and looked at the funds in my checking account. I called Ronald on the prepaid phone.

"Ronald!" I exclaimed. "Did you transfer ALL of Father's money?"

Ronald laughed.

"That didn't make a dent, Jane," Ronald stated, "but it includes proceeds from your house and it's after taxes. I hope that will last a while. The less we communicate, the safer we will be."

"That should be more than enough if I can get back to work," I declared.

"I took that into consideration," Ronald responded.

With the large sum Ronald bestowed on me, I could buy a car and put a good down payment on a house. In a few hours, I drove off a car lot in a different car with a different license plate. It took a few hours more to look at available houses and it was disheartening because I like my old house and neighborhood. Neighbors were important, not because I wanted to socialize, but because they were nosy and would report unusual activity. A gated community looked good to me so I contacted a realtor who was going to meet me the next day.

BT called saying the car was sold and we needed to arrange a time to receive the money and transfer the title. He also wanted me to come to Patty's birthday party or, at least, Patty wanted me to.

At BT's house, balloons were hanging on the front porch and the living room was full of adults, children and pets. Patty ran to greet me followed by BT. He said my name to the crowd and he rattled off theirs. Ushering me through the dining room with settings for several people, he took me into his office. As we discussed arrangements to transfer the car, I suggested a power of attorney would make it easier. BT thought so, too, and he brought in one of his guests who was a notary.

With that business done, he took me to greet Ruth who was filling a large bowl of spaghetti. Some ladies came in ready to take it from her along with sauce, salad and bread. BT pulled bottles of wine out of a cabinet, handed them to me and pointed to the dining room. The ladies were talking about who would sit where and if there were enough seats. One of them took the wine from me and filled glasses.

"Why don't you sit here?" one of the smaller, older ladies suggested.

Moving to the seat, I was glad to be out of the way and watch the hustle-bustle. Bursts of laughter were exploding in the living room and kitchen. In a few minutes, the ladies were escorting children and men to their places. BT and Ruth sat down, everyone settled down and they gave thanks.

Although I was asked a few questions, most of the time I was observing their interactions and listening to their stories. After the cake was eaten and presents were opened, everyone said "Good night." As I said my "good night", with BT, Ruth, Patty and Matthew looking warmly at me, I was a little sad that I was leaving them to go to a luxurious hotel alone.

Chapter 5

The realtor, a young woman, who looked like she stepped out of a real-estate TV commercial, picked me up at the hotel entrance in a family van with two empty car seats in the back. Two houses were available in the gated community and she thought one of them had just been reduced. After touring both, I chose the one that seemed the most secure. She sent an offer and we went to a coffee shop.

BT texted me that the blue, gas-guzzling car belonged to Dennis Cliff, the one accused of manslaughter. Fearing Dennis knew where I was staying, I decided not to return to the hotel. Fortunately, I had the laptop with me. I also decided to break every pattern I could think of like getting new credit card numbers, getting a new phone with a new number and changing my bank account. The ultimate break was quitting my job, the most difficult decision.

When the realtor left, I looked for the nearest five star hotel and headed that direction. Like before, I went to the shops, bought toiletries and clothing and generously tipped the porter. The next morning, I made a spa appointment, changed my checking account, requested new credit cards then bought a new phone. I texted BT the new number. Back at the hotel, I looked on-line for a high-end interior designer. Though I wasn't going to spend the amount of money that they would like, they tended to be discreet which I needed right now.

The designer was available to meet the next day and it was supper time so I decided to eat in the hotel's restaurant. Seated next to a window which overlooked a golf course, I studied the menu and gave my choices to the waiter including a fruity alcohol drink. As the waiter walked away, I was stunned to see Margaret, Jeff and the tall twin with no name, walk into the restaurant. I turned away from them looking at the golf course and I could see their reflection in the window. They were seated across from me with one table between us.

When the waiter returned with my drink, I told him I wasn't feeling well and asked if he would make my order to go. He said he would of course and I took a gulp of my drink. The Hilledebrands were engaged in conversation and I felt sure there was no reason they would recognize me if they looked my way. Glancing nervously toward the kitchen hoping to see the waiter soon, I finished the drink. When I saw my waiter with a bag approaching, I got up to meet him. So eager to leave without being noticed, I tripped and fell into the waiter. He was pushed back into a table that spilled everyone's drinks. The guests let out a yell and of course the entire restaurant was looking at us.

Apologizing profusely, practically in tears, I tried to help the waiter and the guests. All of them were graciously forgiving and the waiter suggested that I could pay at the register. I tipped the waiter more than generously and bought a large gift certificate asking him to give it to my victims. As I left the restaurant, I glanced back at the Hilledebrands and the twin with no name was staring at me. It's times like this when you wish you could discover a portal to another world or better yet a time machine. My destination would be, you guessed it, my car on that dark road that night.

The next day, the interior designer, Martin, an older, slender male in gold pants and beige jacket drove his luxury car into the driveway of my new home in the gated community. As we toured each room, he declared what he liked and didn't like and made his extravagant suggestions. Then the budget I gave him brought him back to reality. He did nothing to hide his disappointment and we looked at furnishings online. We made an appointment to have my choices moved in a week from today. Not wanting to hang around for a week with little to do, I texted BT about my leaving on vacation. He said it was fine and told me when I should be back. Walking into the hotel lobby, I was shocked to see one of the twins standing there. Whether it was Dennis or 'No-Name', I had no idea. Not that it mattered, I didn't want to talk to either. Returning to the parking garage, I rushed to my car. As I got in the driver's seat, the twin stood in the parking garage door, looking around for my car, I assumed. I thought I was able to pull away before he saw me. It seemed I had no choice but to go to the airport, and at a light, I asked my phone for directions. The gas-guzzling blue car sped in front of me, going north. Wouldn't it figure that I needed to turn that direction to get to the airport?

Going straight through the light, I turned north. The blue gas-guzzling car passed me again going south. I could see him in the mirror and he had his blinker light on to turn left. That meant he was turning around. With an immediate right turn, I pulled into a parking garage. Pulling a ticket out of the kiosk, I drove to the top floor. Getting out of my car, I rushed to the wall where I could see the entrance. I felt sure he could not have turned around fast enough to see me pull in here. Now I believed the evil twin, Dennis, knew what kind of car I had so I was afraid to drive it and afraid to have it towed home. What a mess!

BT was my only option and I hated to take him away from his family.

"BT", I started, "I'm stuck in a parking garage."

"Stuck?" he repeated with concern.

"I think Dennis was at the hotel," I explained. "He tried to follow me to the airport."

"Dear, Lord!" BT exclaimed.

BT started talking to someone in the room.

"I'm taking Ruth to the hospital," BT stated.

"Oh, no!", I stammered. "I..I mean..."

"It's okay," BT responded. "Come to my house. My mother is here with the children."

"But Dennis..." I began.

"Dennis wouldn't dare come to my house," BT assured me.

This plan was a relief to me because I would be with other people and BT could eventually take me to the airport. Again, I'm without a toothbrush.

BT's mother, Myra, the shorter, older lady who had seated me at Patty's birthday party, welcomed me like we were best friends. Patty bounded into the room to greet me with little Matthew following. The house was filled with something good cooking; maybe brownies.

"Mom is having a baby girl!" Patty announced with excitement.

"I heard," I cooed, smiling.

"It's coming out of her stomach," Patty explained seriously.

"Really?" I feigned amazement. "I wonder how it got in there?"

I wasn't expecting her answer.

"God put it there, of course," she answered firmly.

"Of course," I agreed, nodding with a smile.

Loud footsteps on the front porch made me jump and look. It was David Stone, the Hilledebrand's lawyer.

"Uncle Dave!" Patty yelled running to the door; Matthew following.

David picked her up, hugging her tightly as she hugged him back then he did the same with Matthew who was waiting his turn. Patty repeated her announcement about the baby; they talked about it for a few minutes. He asked them to draw him a picture which sent both of them running into another room. Then he walked to the couch across from me and sat down.

"Miss Fortner," he greeted in his deep, deep voice.

He was a little taller than me, in his fifties maybe, tan, and the muscles showing through his striped cotton knit shirt had to be the result of regular workouts.

"Hello," I greeted back studying him.

"BT told me about Dennis," he relayed. "I'm sorry you're going through this."

"Not as sorry as I am, believe me," I sighed. "I'm not in a good place right now."

"I realize that," he consoled. "You were in the wrong place at the wrong time, I'm afraid."

"So true," I agreed.

There was a pause.

"I assume you didn't find the phone," I ventured.

"No," he answered shaking his head solemnly.

"Was there nothing in the cloud?" I suggested.

He chuckled, sat back and crossed his ankle over his knee revealing his worn, leather cowboy boots.

"I know what you mean by 'the cloud,'" he began, "but I don't understand it."

"Most people don't," I responded.

Uncomfortable with what I was thinking, I said it anyway because of this horrible situation.

"How good are your technicians?" I probed.

That took him aback.

"As good as most, I suppose," he replied cautiously. "Why?"

"I have computer experience, you know," I explained. "Could I look for the video?"

David shifted and looked down.

"I don't know," he finally answered. "I need to check with my colleagues."

Myra came in and David stood up. They hugged.

"Are you staying for dinner?" Myra invited.

David hesitated then looked at me.

"That would be a pleasure, Ma'am," David responded.

Dinner was roast beef with potatoes and green beans - so much better than restaurant food and I was right about the brownies. The children kept conversation going about school, Sunday school, and their friends. David laughed easily with them and spurred their conversation with questions and challenges. I liked watching him.

We took dishes into the kitchen and Myra rinsed pans and dishes then handed them to me to put in the dishwasher.

"David is a widow," she mentioned. "I don't think he is seeing anyone."

Her statement surprised me.

"Really?" was my only response.

Normally, when people made hints like this, I would find a reason to walk away from the conversation. In this situation, I was trapped.

"You were watching him, you know," Myra continued.

"You're right," I laughed. "He's so good with the children."

A replay of my father talking and laughing with me ran through my mind.

"He is," Myra agreed. "He is *genuinely* good with them."

She stressed the word 'genuinely' as though she knew I was offended at fake behavior or facades. David appeared at the door.

"Great dinner, Myra," he declared, "like always."

She laughed.

"Jane needs a ride to the airport," Myra offered.

I stiffened wishing she hadn't said that. He hesitated a minute glancing at me then at Myra.

"I can take her," David responded then looked at me.

My face burned with embarrassment and I was hoping it wasn't too red.

"It's late," I stammered, wishing I could withdraw.

"It would be a great help to BT," Myra added.

I wanted to look to Heaven and scream, "Why did I lose control of my life?" Instead, I agreed with Myra that it would help BT. She held out her arms and I let her hug me. Patty and Matthew were still drawing. David yelled at them that he was ready to go and they ran to him with pictures. He praised their artwork then they handed pictures to me. I praised them as well.

David took a step toward the door and said he would carry my luggage. Showing him my laptop and purse, I stated there was nothing else. His huge four-door red truck matched his cowboy boots and deep, deep voice. Something that wasn't Bach blared on his radio when he started the car. Quickly turning down the volume, he apologized.

"You're good," I quipped.

"So you're taking a trip?" David asked. "If you don't mind me asking. It's not a lawyer question."

"No problem," I reassured. "With no job and my house isn't ready, there's not much to do here. I can visit some favorite places; maybe lay on a beach somewhere."

He thought for a minute.

"You don't know where you're going?" he asked with surprise.

"Probably Hawaii," I answered. "It's beautiful, I love the tours to the volcanos, it's too expensive for Dennis to follow me there..."

I laughed at my little joke. He was looking at me with concern. That made me want to feel his strong arms around me so I could cry. I missed my father.

"I'm impressed you can make a joke," he complimented. "A lot of people would be getting drunk or taking meds."

"I'm good at facades," I explained. "It's necessary when you're a computer help desk manager."

"Or a lawyer," he agreed as we pulled into the airport.

Like I would expect from a gentleman, he got out of the truck, opened my door and helped me out.

"I can go in with you," he offered.

"No, not necessary," I assured him. "I traveled with my parents for a lot of years; I'm an experienced traveler."

He extended his hand that engulfed mine. His grip was as strong as I expected it would be. I watched him get into the truck and he waved before he drove off. I headed to Hawaiian Airlines.

Chapter 6

With a morning view of the beautiful, endless, blue-green ocean and the calming sound of waves hitting the shores, I woke refreshed after the long airplane ride. The view was worth the expensive suite which I took because it was available. Ronald would not be pleased at the extravagance. Everything I needed for coffee was provided and I sipped a cup on the veranda but my stomach was begging me for food. Because I didn't want to shower just yet, I ordered room service. Another extravagance Ronald would abhor.

It felt so good to relax; I mean really relax. Dennis and the Hilledebrands were an ocean away. No-one was calling me to get their computer started. Unfortunately, the money Ronald sent me wouldn't support this lifestyle the rest of my life.

A knock on the door brought me some sweet rolls and fruit. Taking my time, I formed an agenda. If I was going to the beach, I wanted a swim suit with flip-flops and I wanted to book some tours. The hotel had events planned that looked interesting. The end of this retreat caused by the trial date was the only dark spot in my near future.

It surprised me and worried me a little when someone knocked on my door. Looking out the peep hole, it was a delivery of a floral bouquet. Opening the door a little, I handed out a tip and took the flowers. The card was signed with a QR code. This was Ronald reaching out to me. In Hawaii? Scanning the QR code, it required a password and I guessed it was the same as the laptop. "Meet at helicopter port 2pm" was the message. I assumed this was the port that my parents always used. In a rush now, I showered, got dressed and got in a cab. With minutes to spare, I was relieved that someone reserved me a seat although I was the only passenger.

The helicopter flew over the infinite, blue ocean, black volcanic landscape and then mountains covered by a carpet of green, cut with waterfalls plunging for miles. Finally a brown, smoking volcano came into view. Unlike previous tours I had experienced, the pilot landed and handed me earphones. I put them on then I heard Ronald.

"Jane," Ronald said. "There's not much time."

"Ronald?" I whispered.

Maybe 500 feet from me, looking at the helicopter, Ronald was leaning on a walker; not at all the rigorous, strong man I once knew. I knew he was going to say what I didn't want to hear.

"I'm dying," he stated flatly. "It doesn't matter now if they find me.

He chuckled.

"I'm free, at last," he added as he coughed for several seconds. "And you will never have to work again."

Pain, like an electric shock, shot through my body and tears flowed freely. The money didn't matter and I didn't notice a young woman, maybe 20 years old, walking to the helicopter.

"Machi is walking toward you," Ronald said. "Your father is her father."

I turned into a lifeless brick at that moment with my eyes glued on the young woman. She was Asian, petite, in a sleeveless flowered blouse and blue capris. No shoes.

"Ronald..." I started in anguish but he interrupted.

"Your father had a mistress and this is their child," he explained. "I raised her after your father's death. I can't imagine what you're feeling right now..."

He coughed for several seconds.

"My dying wish is that you feel compassion," he finished.

Looking at him, he was looking at me. I put my hand on the window, pretending I was touching him.

"I will," I whispered, as I used my shirt for a tissue.

"I knew you would," Ronald stated. "Do some good with the money. I always loved you as though you were my own."

"I know," I whispered.

"I'm free now," he added. "Be happy for me."

"Okay," I smiled, although he was asking the impossible.

Machi got into the helicopter. The pilot reached for the earphones to take them from me, made sure Machi was secure and the helicopter rose into the air. Ronald was looking up at me then he crumpled to the ground. The people who saw him ran to him. I was hoping, no praying, that he crumpled due to his illness and not a bullet.

The ride back to the main island was quiet. Staring out the window, tears flowed freely. I didn't look at Machi; I didn't want to acknowledge her presence. She was my father's illegitimate child; the product of my father's adultery.

"You are Jane?" she finally asked in a tiny voice.

With a deep sigh, I summoned my computer manager, happy face facade.

"Yes, and you are Machi?" I mimicked, turning away from the window toward her.

"And your father is my father?" she continued.

"I guess so," I agreed.

"I didn't know I had a sister," Machi declared. "Ronald told me today."

"I didn't know either," I repeated. "I also just found out today."

"When Ronald saw you were in Hawaii, he rushed me on the plane with him," Machi explained.

"Oh?" I responded, interested.

"We raced to the airport," she relayed. "I never saw him hurry so fast."

She sighed and looked out the window.

"My friends won't know what happened to me," she whispered. "My boss won't know..."

Compassion did fill my heart at that moment. She was alone and without a toothbrush, same as me.

"When we get to the hotel, can you call them?" I suggested.

Her face brightened and she smiled broadly.

"Could we?" she asked with hope.

"Of course," I assured her. "Of course."

At the hotel, we went to the shops to get her some clothes, shoes and toiletries. It was maddening to me that her tiny figure allowed her to buy from the junior's department. Her choices were tasteful and she looked for bargains. She got only essentials in the expensive shops and insisted we go to a discount store as soon as possible. Without her knowing it, she was winning my heart. We easily agreed on which laptop to buy and a prepaid phone. I promised to buy her a real phone when we got home. In the hotel room, it was gratifying to see that she not only knew how to start the computer but to also set it up. In no time, she was connected to her friends. She called her boss though she wasn't sure what to say. I told her to explain that her guardian died unexpectedly and she was with a sister. He wanted to know when she would return and started to scold her which was upsetting her.

"Ask him if he can hold on a minute," I suggested.

She put him on hold.

"You don't have to work," I informed her.

She stared at me blankly.

"What will I do?" she asked with amazement.

"Whatever you want!" I laughed.

With a stunned look, she spoke to her boss.

"My sister says I don't have to work," she repeated.

His voice rose to a hysteric level and we both started laughing. We listened to him rant for a minute or two then he paused.

"So, I'm resigning today," she finished and ended the call.

She leaped to her feet and started dancing around the room.

"I don't have to work!" she chanted. "I don't have to work!"

It was fun watching her dance with joy. I was so glad she had called her boss from a prepaid phone because he would never be able to bother her again.

On my laptop, I bought tickets for tours and events, assuming Machi would accompany me as I had accompanied my mother. Machi was engaged with her friends. When she finally took a break from her laptop, I asked if she was hungry and mentioned I had booked some tours. To my shock, she replied that she was going to a party.

"Who do you know in Hawaii?" I wondered, with amazement.

"I have friends who know friends," she answered flatly, like it was a silly question, then she closed the door to her room and I could hear the shower.

This was so completely opposite from me, I could barely comprehend that she would go to be with a group of people she didn't know in a place she didn't know. This situation was also uncomfortably foreign. In my past, my mother made the agenda and I followed. Before the accident, I made my agenda and followed it. Now, I wasn't sure how to proceed. Should I head for the restaurant, which I wanted to do, or should I wait to tell Machi where I'm going? How annoying! Walking to the veranda, I flopped in a chair, pouting, feeling powerless as I waited for this stranger to emerge from her room. My stomach was yelling at me. The shower stopped and I bounded to her door, knocked three times, and said her name with anger, 'Machi'!

She opened the door, wrapped in a towel, and looked up at me, innocently. Realizing my anger was out of place and my adult self taking over, I told her I was going to supper and then to a concert. She nodded.

"I want you to have my phone number," I stated.

She turned away to get her phone and I did as well. She gave me the number of the prepaid phone which I called. We both took a moment to set up the contact.

"Be careful," I offered. "I wish you would come with me to a concert."

"Don't worry" she smiled then she laughed. "You're like Uncle Ron. He always worried."

"A key to the room is on the counter," I advised. "Don't forget it."

She closed the door and I could easily imagine Ronald being very worried. There was no doubt in my mind that a body guard went everywhere with Machi, probably without her knowledge. That made me wonder, for the first time, if he had a body guard following me.

On returning from the concert, after midnight, Machi's door was open and the room was dark. Again, anger rose in me and, again, I didn't know what to do. Should I call her? Should I care? I decided not to care with the help of some alcohol. Planning to take a small bottle from the bar, I gasped when I saw it was empty. Either the bar was never stocked, very unlikely, or Machi had cleaned it out. Imagining how much that would cost, I stormed out of the suite toward the hotel's lounge.

Choosing a table, the waiter quickly brought water and I ordered an alcohol drink and a light snack. Many tables were occupied and a few couples were dancing to music from a juke box. Sipping my drink, waiting for it's calming effect, a man said my name. The man, in a brown leather airman jacket, was bent down slightly, waiting for me to respond. Looking up into his intense green eyes, I responded with a 'yes'.

"I'm Brad Newman," he announced. "Ronald's son."

Without asking, he sat down. He seemed to know I would not have given him permission to join me had he asked.

"Ronald's son," I repeated lamely, crossing my arms.

With a groan, Brad pulled out a wallet from his inside jacket pocket and showed me a picture of Ronald and my father with a young boy and a young girl.

"The girl resembles Machi," I observed, "but how can I know that is you?"

He sighed deeply with a look of irritation.

"You impressed me this afternoon when I delivered the flowers," he offered. "You kept your body behind the door and hid most of your face. Nice tip by the way."

He smiled which showed crows feet around his eyes. His brown hair was cut in short military style. Keeping silent, I waited for more proof. He got the hint.

"My father's dying wish was that you feel compassion," he relayed. "You responded, 'I will.'"

I gasped.

"You're the helicopter pilot?" I guessed.

He nodded. The waiter stopped by and Brad ordered a drink then helped himself to some of my snack. I chuckled at his audacity. Now accepting he was telling the truth, questions flooded my mind.

"How did Ronald know I was in Hawaii?" was my first question.

"Really?" Brad smirked. "Really? You don't know that answer? I thought you were a computer wiz."

"Humor me," I demanded with disdain.

"He set up your bank account," Brad answered leaving off the 'stupid woman' apparent in his tone. "He set up alerts if you spent large amounts of money. First class tickets to Hawaii aren't cheap!"

I laughed at myself then made a mental note to change bank accounts as soon as possible.

"Of course," I affirmed. "That would be like him."

"When he was pronounced terminally ill, he vowed to take Machi to you," Brad recounted.

"Where is her mother?" I asked.

"Cancer took her life," Brad replied. "Actually, it happened close to your mother's death."

"No wonder Father died soon after," I whispered.

Brad took a gulp of his drink, ate some more of my snack then ordered another drink.

"Hawaii was a perfect place to contact you," Brad continued. "Travel here is expensive and takes a lot of time, compared to most places. The chances of being followed were slim. He was thanking God for the opportunity."

"How did you get here?" I wondered.

"Private jet," Brad answered leaning back in the chair with an air of pride. "I'm a pilot."

Nodding with understanding, my brain argued about which subject to approach first, 'God' or 'being followed'.

"Did he believe in God?" I ventured. "He never mentioned God."

"When he got sick, he talked more about God," Brad answered flatly. "Chaplains visited him in the hospital and read the Bible to him. I think he started praying about us, his family, you know?"

I nodded with understanding.

"And was he still being followed?" I questioned with fear. "My father was terrified of being followed."

"You know why, don't you?" Brad asked with some arrogance.

"They were accused of spying?" I responded.

"Right, accused of spying," he affirmed.

"What were you told?" I wondered.

The new drink arrived.

"Our fathers were computer geniuses," Brad started. "They built systems and networks for hundreds, maybe a thousand, companies and organizations around the world. Some of them were government organizations - foreign government offices."

He gulped his drink and finished my snack. His tapered physique did not match consumption of this amount of alcohol and food.

"One of the dignitaries in one of those foreign government offices accused them of stealing and selling secrets," Brad continued. "Friends got them out of the country before they were jailed. After that they never ventured on foreign soil. An old warrant for their arrest is still posted on Interpol with a reward."

"A reward?" I blurted. "I never heard that."

"It's not a huge reward but bounty-hunters do exist, you know," he winked.

"It can't affect us now, though, right?" I hoped. "Since both of them are gone?"

"Only if someone wants the money back," he stated as he stood up.

"Oh, great!" I exclaimed. "Thanks for that word of encouragement."

He laughed as he took a step toward the exit.

"Wait!" I entreated, holding onto his solid arm. "Did Ronald die of his illness when he collapsed today?"

"He was near death," Brad responded. "I made it to the hospital to say goodbye."

"But was it the illness that killed him?" I pressed.

Brad looked at me with question then leaned down with one hand on the back of the chair and the other on the table, as though he were shielding me.

"It was the illness," he stated and he put his hand on my shoulder. "My father worried about how this...this 'hiding' affected you. He often expressed hope that you would find rest from it."

Moments after Brad disappeared through the lounge exit, I realized his drinks were on my tab and I, again, laughed at his audacity. Back in the hotel room, Machi was still out and it was 2 AM. Sitting on the veranda, not sleepy, I scrolled through my phone for interesting articles and videos. The sound of the ocean was relaxing. Though I hadn't looked at my bank account, I knew I now had enough money to stay here the rest of my life but I also knew that was a huge waste of money. My scrolling changed to homes for sale, worldwide. Thankful that my eyes finally got heavy enough for sleep, I crawled into bed.

The next morning, my phone woke me, way too early. Machi was calling.

"I need a ride," Machi stated factually. "I'm hungry and everyone is sleeping. I don't have money. I need to shower."

With a smirk at her audacity, somewhat like Brad's, I made her a family member on a credit card.

"You should have an invitation to..." I started.

"I see it," she quickly interrupted. "Thank you. I can get a cab now. Thank you."

She hung up and, though miffed she was out all night, I was also relieved she was alright. Deciding to get up, I ordered breakfast, made coffee and sat on the veranda. Thoughts of going home entered my mind because I didn't want Machi going out again all night. She needed a routine that would keep her safe and out of trouble. She needed a job or maybe she could go back to school. Machi then came through the door carrying a bag of fast food heading toward her room.

"Machi!" I blurted. "Can we talk?"

She walked toward me and sat down, looking at me obediently. She didn't look like she had been up all night.

"Did you take all the liquor out of the bar?" was my first question.

"I took it to the party," she answered glibly with a shrug. "You have to take something to the party!"

"Of course," I nodded, very relieved she didn't drink it all, then, my second question. "I'd like to go home. Are you coming with me?"

"Yes, of course," she agreed quickly. "When are you leaving? Can I shower?"

Her flexibility was amazing and took me by surprise.

"You have no plans today?" I wondered.

"I'm going home with you," she responded with a laugh as though I had forgotten the plan.

When someone knocked on the door, she bounded up to respond; I gave her money for a tip. Breakfast had arrived. She rolled the cart to me and pulled her fast food breakfast out of the bag, put it on a plate and moved her chair closer to the cart.

"We eat together?" she suggested. "Our first breakfast as a family."

"Yes," I agreed with a smile, amazed that a few weeks ago, a scene like this would have been incomprehensible to me.

While she showered, I cancelled the tours, made airline reservations and also got in the shower. We had three hours to get to the airport. Putting on my last clean outfit, I contemplated what to do with our clothes: buy a suitcase or just leave them. As if reading my mind, Machi came in with the same question.

"I think we should leave them," I suggested.

"Leave them!" Machi exclaimed with shock, just as Ronald would have.

"With the cost of a new suitcase, we can buy six more outfits," I reasoned.

"Who needs a suitcase?" Machi exclaimed as she left my room.

She brought in her outfits and folded everything. Laying a pair of my slacks on the bed, she arranged the folded items on top of the slacks, then rolled them up like a sleeping bag. Somehow she used tee shirts to make it into a backpack. Her creativity was impressive and I told her so.

Arriving at the airport with time to spare, we found a coffee shop close to the gate.

"What do you want to do with your life?" I ventured.

"What do you want to do with yours?" she responded.

I sighed wanting her to answer me, but I answered instead.

"Well, I traveled a lot as a child so I don't want to travel," I started. "I had a job helping people with their computers and I liked that job. So I think I want to find a job like that."

"What happened to your job?" she wondered. "Did you tell your boss you don't have to work, like me?"

She laughed.

"Oh, that is a complicated story," I answered.

She looked at me, and, with a deep sigh, I explained what was waiting for me when I got home.

"Oh, no!" she blurted with empathy. "It's just like Father and Uncle Ron! You are innocent yet you are being accused and followed!"

Remembering what Brad said about a bounty, I wondered what Machi knew.

"Do you know who Father was afraid of?" I ventured.

"Not exactly," Machi began. "He was not home much. It was Uncle Ron more than Father who was nervous."

"But why was he nervous?" I pressed.

"I think," she began looking away like she was trying to remember, "I think he had been under arrest? In some country?"

She shook her head.

"I heard Uncle Ron talk to his son, Brad, sometimes but never to me," Machi explained.

"I saw Brad last night," I revealed. "He said there is a bounty."

"A bounty, yes," Machi agreed. "That's what Uncle Ron was afraid of. You saw Brad?"

"Yes, I was in the lounge and he was there," I answered.

"So that's why he left the party," Machi responded. "I didn't know he was coming here to talk to you."

Machi smiled.

"Now I know why Father was gone all the time!" she announced. "He was with you and your mother!"

Though, in my mind, this should have made her angry, she laughed.

"Did you know they weren't married?" I asked with concern.

"Oh, they were married," Machi insisted. "They had wedding pictures. Brad was the ring-bearer."

The shock of her words thrust me back in my chair.

"Our father had two wives, Machi," I blurted. "Two families!"

She nodded like I was talking about the weather.

"It's good that he was rich, yes?" she offered.

I had to agree with that.

Our flight was announced and we walked toward the gate. Being first class, we were seated quickly. It was noon in Hawaii and about 6 PM at home. It would be about 6 AM when we landed. Expecting to be exhausted, I made a hotel reservation several miles from the gated community, the Gladstone Hotel and the restaurant where I last saw the gas-guzzling car. My plan was to get a cab to the hotel and let my body adjust however it wanted.

Machi was attempting to connect to her friends which would be difficult when flying over the Pacific Ocean. She finally put on a movie and I watched it with her. We both liked making comments on the acting, the wardrobe and any flaws in the storyline. We laughed a lot; it was quite entertaining.

Just as I planned, the cab took us to a hotel many miles from the trauma waiting for me. Machi was quietly trying to connect to her friends and I was liking the scenery we were passing. Though I would not have called the homes 'wealthy' they were substantial. Many were old homes, well maintained, and miles of land was surrounded with fence painted white as though they were horse farms.

"Are these horse farms?" I asked the cab driver.

"Well, I wouldn't call them horse farms exactly," he answered, "though I do see horses on this land. The land with white fences is owned by the Francisco Farms Restaurants."

"Oh, wow!" I marveled.

Everyone I knew was aware of the Francisco Farms Restaurants. They claimed their food was raised and grown locally. It looks like this is where it came from.

The hotel looked like a college campus, quite impressive. Machi and I walked into the luxurious lobby with our laptop bags and the tiny bundle of clothes. It made a funny picture in my mind. We were escorted into our room and I glanced at the shopping area, looking forward to a few hours in the spa.

Though there was a nice balcony facing a forest, it was drab compared to the beautiful Hawaiian beach. Machi was sitting on the couch laughing at something on her laptop and I marveled how she appeared to be unaffected by what had occurred the last 48 hours. Getting her settled somewhere was becoming very important to me. Thinking of the house in the gated community, I wondered now if that was a good choice for her. She never answered my question about what she wanted to do.

A brochure, lying on the desk caught my eye. It was published by a local community club and focused on area organizations and attractions. The Francisco Farms and the hundreds of jobs they provided were listed as well as a local Christian college. An idea was forming that I might want to move into this area; that a Christian college would be attended by moderate people rather than the extremes found in secular campuses.

"Machi," I called and she looked up. "Did you go to college?"

She shook her head and looked at her laptop again.

"Would you be interested?" I offered. "It's a great place to make lifetime friends."

She left her laptop and flopped in a chair across from me.

"Do you want me to go?" she questioned. "I'll go if you want me to."

"Is there something else you want to do?" I pressed.

"I don't know what I want to do," Machi answered with frustration. "Uncle Ron always asked me this."

"I want you to go, then," I concluded. "I went to college because Father wanted me to."

She nodded and sighed then returned to her laptop. Opening my laptop, I clicked the link to my bank account. When the amount came into view, I gasped at the number of digits in the available balance. I wasn't an accountant, but I knew that much money would have to be managed wisely or taxes would consume it. A new link was also available - Machi's account with the same number of digits.

A couple of emails were posted. One from Ronald with a short message saying 'good-bye'. A second was from an attorney. I called him.

"This is Jane Fortner," I began. "May I speak to Ben Cortland?"

"Miss Fortner," he greeted. "Thank you for calling."

"Of course," I stated.

There was a pause.

"You seem to be alright," he ventured.

"You mean because of Ronald's death?" I wondered.

"Yes and Machi?" he continued.

"It was shocking of course," I answered with a quiver in my voice. "It will haunt me my entire life, I'm sure. And Machi..."

I looked at her laughing at her laptop.

"Machi is extremely resilient," I explained. "She would fit wherever you put her."

Ben sighed as though relieved.

"I've worked with your father and Ron for many years," Ben offered. "I've helped them with patents, investments, real estate, estate planning..."

"No need to pitch to me, Mr. Cortland," I interrupted. "If Ronald trusted you; I trust you. I can tell you now that I want the money transferred to different accounts. Brad told me..."

"Brad!" Ben exclaimed. "When did you see Brad?"

"The day Ronald died," I replied. "He came to the hotel. What's wrong?"

"I begged Ronald not to involve Brad," Ben revealed. "I don't trust him."

"I don't know him that well but I want the account transferred because of him," I continued.

Relaying to him that Brad was aware of the alerts Ronald had set up, I told him how I wanted the accounts changed, I specified the vpn

I wanted him to use and the back-up company. He said he would text me when it was done. My next call was to Martin, the interior designer, asking him to hold the furniture until further notice. He ranted about the storage charges and I promised to pay any additional costs. Lastly, I made a spa appointment and Machi agreed to go with me this time.

The next morning, my body was feeling normal and, though not liking the thought, I was willing at least to face the realities of my life. Ordering a car, I took Machi to get a real phone and showed her how to disable the prepaid phone. Then, I told my phone to direct me to the college. The campus was charming and some of the buildings were built in the 17th or 18th century. The neighborhood surrounding the college was also charming and many homes were like historic landmarks. All of it was attractive to me. A three story Victorian on a corner lot was for sale. I liked that it was distanced from the other homes yet part of the neighborhood. Pulling into the drive way, I liked that a garage was connected to the house but still looked like part of the original architecture. My young realtor was shocked that I was selling the house in the gated community and was looking at another one miles away. We made an appointment to tour the home the next day.

Getting a text that the bank accounts were set up, I called an auditing company and made arrangements to have our accounts audited quarterly. From articles I read in computer magazines, this auditing company was top-rated and used by the richest people in the world.

Back at the hotel, I put chicken in the oven, Machi connected to her laptop and I threw our bundle of clothes in the washing machine. All of this was feeling very comfortable, even in a hotel suite, when BT called. I sighed.

"Hi, BT," I greeted. "How is Ruth?"

"Ruth is fine, the baby is fine," BT answered. "How are you?"

"You won't believe how I am," I quipped and I told him who was staying with me.

"Un-believable!" BT ranted. "I'd expect to read this in a fiction novel."

"No kidding!" I agreed.

BT reviewed the court date, time and courtroom number. He reviewed the case and their strategy:

"Based on Margaret and Jeff's testimony, Dennis has been accused of manslaughter." BT began. "Dennis denies the charges but his unique car was caught on tape parked beside Jill's car at the building where Jill said the attempted rape occurred. Dennis cannot account for the time his car was gone from that building until he arrived at his apartment around 9 PM that night, which was also caught on tape. Bailey wants the jury to believe that you were chasing Jill and not Dennis. She has no proof that you ever met Dennis or Jill or any of the family. David will impress upon the jury that there is no proof. In a sane world, it should be obvious that you are not in any way involved other than you had concern for the victim of an accident."

Chapter 7

Machi and I had moved into the Victorian and she was attending the Christian college. In no time, she was busy socializing with new friends including attending church on Sunday. I'm not sure she realized that church had any significance other than her friends went so she went.

At 8 AM on a Monday morning, I was sitting in the back row of the courthouse. Jeff and Margaret entered the courtroom and, like they did before, they sat in the first row. The twin with no name also entered and walked to Margaret and Jeff but, when he turned to take a seat, he glanced at me, and nodded his head my direction. While I was happy to be acknowledged, he needed to be reminded that we were not supposed to make contact.

BT entered and sat in front of me. I told him what No-Name had done and he grimaced.

"He's a naturally friendly guy," BT explained. "His name is 'Dean', by the way. He told David about your incident in the restaurant."

"Oh, no!" I exclaimed, rolling my eyes feeling my face redden.

Bailey walked into the courtroom with Dennis and they sat at the defendant's table.

"By the way," I remembered. "How did Dennis know I was at that hotel?"

BT shifted and sighed.

"How can I put this gently?" BT wondered, pretending to search his memory. "Well, I can't. Margaret is a bit of a flake."

"A flake?" I chuckled involuntarily.

"She doesn't have common sense, I guess is a better description," BT repeated. "Even though Dennis is accused of attempted rape of her daughter, she stays connected to him. She insists we need to forgive him and prayer will change him. I personally think he is really good at deception and pandering."

"And how did he find out?" I re-directed BT back to the subject.

"He was at their house," BT began, "and Margaret made careless comments that you were drunk in the restaurant, falling all over people..."

"What?" I blurted with instantaneous rage.

"Shhh!" BT urged as he looked around.

"How am I going to get out of this mess with statements like that?" I challenged.

"Calm down," BT begged. "We've gone over this."

"If Margaret is forgiving Dennis, who is pressing these charges?" I interrupted.

"Dean," BT replied factually. "Jill was his fiancé."

That answer broke my heart. I looked at 'No-Name' and he glanced up at me at that moment.

"He keeps looking at me!" I declared with anguish.

"I'm not surprised," BT shrugged. "You look just like Jill. He probably can't get over the resemblance."

"That must be causing him a lot of pain," I mused, and I had another reason for this nightmare to be over.

The bailiff called the session to order, announcing the judge and the participants. As before, the two patrolmen and the fireman testified then I was called. David approached me and like before, asked me my name, address and where I worked. After saying my name, I explained that I lost my job because of this case and I gave the address of the house in the gated community, which I still owned. David looked at me with suspicion, but he let it go.

"Before the accident, Miss Fortner," David began, "did you know any of the Cliff family?"

"No," I answered.

"Did you know any of the Hilledebrand family?" he asked.

"No," I answered.

"Do you know them now?" he asked.

"I know *of* them," I answered.

David nodded with a slight smile and winked at me.

"When did you first know *of* them, Miss Fortner," he asked, using my phraseology.

"I first knew of Jill Hilledebrand the night of the accident," I answered.

"What happened that night?" David asked.

I repeated what happened.

"So before that night, you never met Jill and you never met her collie," David repeated.

"That's right," I answered.

David walked to his table and picked up some pictures.

"Your Honor," David said handing pictures to the judge, "These are pictures of Jill Hilledebrand with her collie, named 'Ty.'"

The judge accepted the pictures and David walked back to me.

"When did you meet Margaret and Jeff Hilledebrand?" David asked.

"When they picked up the collie at my house," I answered.

"Why was the collie at your house?" he asked.

"I have no idea," I answered. "He turned up there on his own."

David walked to his table.

"Your Honor, I wish to submit these affidavits from Miss Fortner's neighbors that they witnessed a blue, historic car parked at the curb of Miss Fortner's house on three occasions and, on each occasion, a man was observed leading a collie to Miss Fortner's porch. The description of the man given by all the neighbors matches the defendant."

Gasping, I thought, "Great job, guys!" Bailey had her arms crossed, looking down. Dennis, red-faced, his arm resting on the back of Bailey's chair, leaning too close to her, was saying something that looked like it should be bleeped.

"No further questions, Your Honor," David stated.

"Your witness, Miss Cardell," the judge announced.

"No further questions," Bailey murmured.

Taking a seat behind BT, I patted his shoulder.

"Great job!" I whispered.

"It was all David," BT responded. "He was already livid that Dennis was harassing you and disrupting your life but, after he met you, he was determined to..to rescue you, I guess."

"My hero," I sighed with a smile, putting both hands over my heart and batting my eyes.

We laughed.

"Order in the court!" the judge blurted.

BT wouldn't let me leave the courtroom but I wished I could have. Nothing more about me came up in the trial but Bailey pointed out that the neighbor's description of the man who brought the collie to my house could also have been Dean. Unfortunately, the jury didn't see enough evidence to convict Dennis. As I was complaining to BT that Dennis would be free to harass me, 'No-Name', now 'Dean', stopped at the row where I was sitting. He reached his hand toward me.

"I'm Dean Cliff," he began. "Jill was my fiancé."

Shaking his hand, I was mesmerized that he was looking at me with the same intensity that my father did.

"I'm so sorry," I stammered, forgetting to release his hand.

"No, I'm sorry for everything you've been through," he consoled, not pulling his hand away.

"Thank you," I whispered letting him go; he left.

David walked by.

"David," I blurted and he stopped. "Thank you, thank you, thank you."

He smiled and shook his head.

"All in a day's work, Miss Fortner," he stated, then he left.

BT rose and I shook his hand. He pulled me into a hug.

"Call me anytime," he urged. "And, some of your retainer is left."

"Hang onto it," I advised and he left.

Taking a deep breath, I felt like thanking God this was over though not really sure why I thought he had been involved.

At home, Machi was working on her laptop, surrounded by books, when I walked into the kitchen with bags of food. She greeted me, continued typing for a minute, then walked toward the kitchen.

"How was Court?" she asked.

"Good news and bad news," I teased as I put groceries away. "Good news is David made it very clear to the jury that I was not involved with Dennis; bad news is that Dennis wasn't convicted."

"Oh, no!" Machi declared. "Now he is free to harass you more. What will we do?"

Though I loved that she said "we", a deep sigh escaped.

"I don't want to move," I stated. "I like this house and this little town."

"Me too," Machi agreed.

"We can keep renting different cars every few weeks," I suggested, "so there are no license records he can look up. He doesn't know about you so he doesn't know to look you up. What else?"

"We can pray," Machi blurted.

Why this surprised me, I can't say; she was in a Christian school after all.

"You want to pray?" I asked with hesitation.

"Yes, of course," she urged. "God knows everything. He is the smartest of everyone. He loves us and will protect us."

"But I'm not going to church," I stammered. "Why would he care?"

"He cares about you," Machi responded. "He wants peace for you and joy."

She was looking at me with a longing I didn't understand. This was important to her.

"Okay," I agreed.

She held my hands and closed her eyes.

"Our Heavenly Father," she began, "Jane and I pray to you now about Dennis. You know what he's done, to us and to Jill and Jill's family..."

"And Dean," I added.

"Yes, Dean," Machi repeated. "You know everything, Lord. You know what is best for Dennis and for us. We pray for your will to be done in Dennis and in us."

"And in Dean," I added.

"And in Dean," Machi added. "Amen."

"Amen," I repeated.

We immediately hugged like we never had before.

"You like Dean," Machi teased with an impish smile.

"Oh, I told you that Jill was his fiancé; I feel bad for him," I retorted.

She stared at me smiling.

"That's all, really," I declared. "How could I like someone I've never talked to?"

She returned to her laptop and I prepared chicken to bake.

"I could like him," I dared to think. "I'd love the opportunity."

Chapter 8

The rest of the year was filled with Machi's school and church activities, and the interior designer, Martin, had taken over my life. He talked me into remodeling and updating the Victorian. While I agreed with his ideas, it was terrifying that strangers would have access to my home. Thankfully, he was sympathetic and promised he would use only his best, most trusted associates, which would, of course, cost more and take longer. While I have heard that the love of money is the root of all evil, it is a lot of fun when there is more than enough.

Anyway, their presence made me want to live in a hotel until they were done but I received my first quarterly report from the auditor and the amount of money Machi and I spent was overwhelming. Almost hearing Ronald's objections blaring from his grave, I decided to tough it out.

One night, however, Machi was trying to study and she was frustrated that every room was in some kind of disarray and she felt the dust was making her ill. She plopped down beside me on my bed and asked me if I would agree to her moving in with a friend.

This was a 20-year-old who was not my child asking me this question. A 20-year-old who I liked. A 20-year-old that my father would want me to care about. I shared my dilemma.

"You know I care about you," I began.

"Yes, of course," Machi agreed immediately. "You could have left me in Hawaii."

"Your old enough to make your own decisions," I continued.

"Really?" Machi smiled. "Thank you."

"You know there are bad people who don't care about you," I advised, "like Dennis."

"You worry," Machi responded, "like Uncle Ron."

"And like our father?" I suggested as my face puckered getting ready to cry.

Machi nodded looking sad.

"Father was a good man," Machi practically whispered. "I miss him."

We watched tears stream down each other's faces and embraced.

"I miss him, too," I added.

We both wiped our faces with our shirts.

"Are houses for rent near the college?" I wondered.

Her face immediately brightened with a smile.

"That's a great idea!" she exclaimed. "Can we look tomorrow? No classes tomorrow."

I agreed and we decided to find a movie. She curled up next to me and we found one that was funny and there was a lot to criticize.

The next morning, at breakfast, Machi and I expressed hope that we would find a house. While the choices of houses near the campus weren't so great, a large, well-maintained condominium complex was located a few miles down the road. Driving through the various streets, we were excited to see one for rent. We dialed the number and was told someone could be there soon. As we waited, one of those large, industrial lawn mowers drove onto the street. As it got closer, the driver looked like he might be one of the twins. My heart raced with dread that it was Dennis and hope that it was Dean. The mower passed our car. Though he wore a cap and wrap-around sun glasses, I could see his hair was sandy brown and his nose and mouth looked right. His tank top revealed his tan, muscular shoulders and they looked like the right breadth.

A car pulled up behind us and an elderly man got out then Machi and I met him. The lawn mower had moved to the other side of the street thankfully because, if it was Dennis, I didn't want him to recognize me. I hurried to the front porch and kept my back to the mower. The elderly man wasn't walking fast enough.

The open layout of the condo was pleasing though the kitchen was small. Two bedrooms with two full baths were good. It was going to meet our needs in this situation. The elderly man asked us to follow him to the office to pay deposit and first month's rent and sign a contract. The rent and membership fee was pricey but I knew that's why the complex was well-maintained and not over-run with students.

Before signing the contract, I asked about the lawn maintenance. The manager said a local company was hired and she described everything they were responsible for. Explaining I had seen the man driving the mower, I asked if she knew his name. She said it could be Dennis or Dean. Machi and I both groaned and looked to Heaven.

"What do you want to do?" Machi asked, looking at me with concern.

"Do we run or stand and fight?" I answered.

She grinned widely and I signed the papers. Eager to live a dust-free life, we rented a small moving van to get a few essential pieces of furniture out of the Victorian. While we could have rented furniture, I knew strangers would deliver it and Machi thought it was a waste of money. We deemed the couch, one comfortable chair, the kitchen table with chairs and our beds were essential. Getting them out of the Victorian was easy because of the sliding glass door. Getting them into the condo was a challenge.

Managing to get the couch in, we sat on it for a few minutes, realizing we had nothing in the fridge so we were making a shopping list as we rested. There was a knock on the open door and one of the twins was standing there. A shock that simultaneously felt like dread and excitement shot through me. Asking Machi to step into the bedroom, I hurried to the door.

"Hey," he greeted then interrupted himself. "Well, Jane? Is it?"

He pulled off his sunglasses. He looked at me with my father's intense gaze like he did in the courtroom.

"Dean?" I guessed.

"Yes, Dean Cliff," he answered and I shook his hand.

"I hope you don't mind," he continued. "I thought I could help with this furniture."

"Oh, that would be wonderful!" I exclaimed. "Machi?"

She peaked out the door of the bedroom.

"This is Dean Cliff," I began and I put my hand on his strong arm.

"Oh, Dean!" she blurted and bounded out of the room, all smiles.

"He's going to..." I started but I turned around and he had the bed frame lifted out of the van.

"Where do you want this?" he asked.

Machi pointed into the bedroom she had just emerged from. She looked at me and mouthed the word "Wow!" I nodded in agreement. Both of us marveled as he lifted the items like they were made of paper. In less than 20 minutes, Dean had the essentials in place. Machi and I thanked him profusely telling him he had saved us hours of work. After he left, we both danced around the room so thankful for his help. Then, like we were reading each other's mind, we swooned over the muscles in his arms and what we could see of his chest and back. Then the parent rose in me and told her to be careful. She told me I worry like Uncle Ron.

The coming weeks settled into a comfortable routine. Machi went to school and church and I went to the Victorian to keep an eye on the workers and clean up what I could. They were progressing but it was still going to be months before we could return.

One night, when I pulled into the garage at the condo, the mower was parked in our yard. This I didn't like. Grabbing sacks of groceries, I rushed into the kitchen. One of the twins and Machi were sitting at the kitchen table laughing. Machi had her laptop open and was surrounded by books. Though I was ready to burst with concern and fear, I greeted them calmly and walked to the table standing between them. As soon as the twin looked at me I knew it was Dennis.

"How are you, *Dennis*?" I said with confidence.

Dennis stared at me. Machi turned to me abruptly.

"No!" she cried. "You are mixed up. This is Dean."

I pulled out my phone.

"Okay, we'll see," I challenged and pretended I was looking for a number.

Dennis stood up.

"Got you, Machi!" Dennis blurted. "Got you, good!"

"You are Dennis?" Machi cried as she stood up and pointed to the door. "You have to leave."

I followed him to the door and locked it. This made me want to check all the locks on the windows. Then I made sure the garage door was closed. Machi was watching me.

"I'm sorry," Machi said as I started putting away groceries.

"You did nothing wrong, Machi," I consoled. "He's a deceiver."

"Yes, like the devil," Machi offered.

"Right, just like him," I chuckled.

"How did you know it was Dennis?" she wondered.

"Dean has the same intense gaze as Father," I explained. "Dennis doesn't have it."

"I guess I never noticed," Machi admitted with embarrassment.

This made me realize she had seen Dean after we moved in.

"Has Dean been here before?" I asked with concern and dread.

"A few times," Machi recounted. "Just a short visit. He was curious about my classes at school."

Sitting across from her, I reached for her hands and she gave them to me.

"I don't want you to be here alone anymore," I began. "Does that make sense?"

Machi nodded sadly.

"Will you call me when you leave school and I'll come home, too," I suggested. "Okay?"

"I will," she said.

"I hope you understand that I'm worried for you," I went on. "The wrong decision at our age can ruin our lives."

"Father told me that, too," Machi said with a half smile.

"The virgin lecture?" I whispered as my face reddened.

"Aaaaahhhh!" She laughed loudly throwing back her head. "YES!"

"Virginity is a commodity that some people sell!" I blurted. "Did you know what he was talking about?"

"NO!" she screamed pounding on the table. "For years I wouldn't let a boy come near me thinking I would get sick or ... or something!"

We laughed for several minutes making fun of him and ourselves. When we calmed down, we fixed dinner and ate quietly.

"I know what he meant, now," Machi stated seriously.

"Yes, me too," I agreed, nodding.

"At church, the pastor's wife talked to us," Machi continued quite thoughtfully, like something serious was on her mind. "She said 'our virginity is our gift to our husband like the husband's virginity is a gift to me.' "

We cleaned the kitchen and, while I sat in the living room looking for articles to read or videos to watch, Machi stayed in the kitchen talking to someone. Though I wanted to find out who it was, I decided not to pry. I looked to Heaven.

"God, please help her; please protect her," I whispered.

It was surprising that I felt like I had just done a good thing.

Chapter 9

It had been two years since Ronald's death though it passed without notice by me or Machi. The condo's lease was up and the Victorian was nearly finished, so we moved. Martin's work was stunning and he was so pleased with it, he hired a professional photographer to document the results. As the owner, he wanted to include me dressed in designer clothes and jewels. Merchants agreed to lend these articles in exchange for advertising. The photoshoot took an entire day and I hired a caterer to feed the crew and the merchants who were there to protect their property. Martin was overjoyed when a home and garden magazine published an article about his business that included these pictures.

One Sunday after church, Machi came home in a solemn mood, saying she needed to talk to me. We sat at the kitchen table. As I had done to her a few times, she reached out her hands to me and I took them. Her eyes were teary.

"Dean and I are getting married," Machi stated simply then she waited for me to respond. Tears dripped down her face.

Like I did when I first saw Machi walking toward the helicopter, I turned into a lifeless brick staring at her, gently pulling my hands away.

"How?" I stammered.

"When Dean couldn't see me at the house, he started coming to church," Machi explained.

"But you always came home from church," I declared. "You were always on time."

"We never met anywhere else," Machi replied. "Dean is born-again. He said we can spend the rest of our lives together. He said sitting together in God's presence was good enough for now."

It felt like a building fell on me and I slammed back in my chair.

"I am born-again, too," Machi added.

My brain was numb and no words of response were forming. Few men in my life were ever attractive to me and it was so cruel that this one didn't want me. Machi rose, walked to me and kneeled beside my chair. She was sobbing.

"Can you forgive me?" she begged. "I didn't mean to betray you. I tried to tell Dean it was wrong."

Compassion finally rose in me. I pulled her up and embraced her.

"You did nothing wrong," I consoled. "He wasn't for me, was he? God picked him for you, yes?"

Her sobs turned into shrieks of joy and she danced around the room.

"Praise God! Praise God! Praise God forever!" she yelled then she ran back to me. "Dean is outside. Can he come in?"

"Yes, of course!" I replied. Though her happiness made me happy, I summoned my computer manager facade to cover my disappointment.

Dean stood in the door waiting for me to acknowledge him.

"Dean, please come in," I invited with my best smile.

He reached his hand to me and I took it with both of mine.

"Congratulations!" I declared, way too sincerely.

"Thank you," he smiled humbly and bowed slightly. He was wearing the same dark navy suit as that first day in the courtroom.

"I think she's a lucky girl," I offered.

"I want that to be true," he answered looking at her.

"Right now, I am the happiest girl," she cried as she pulled us into a group hug.

We decided to have Sunday dinner and started preparing it. Machi shared their wedding plans; it would be a fall wedding and I was going to be her maid of honor along with two other bridesmaids. The twins' mother was so excited and was already sharing her ideas. Machi had two years of school left which she wanted to finish and Dean supported her. It hurt to see him look at her knowing she was going to get the attention that I longed for. I missed my father.

Needless to say, the next few months were a whirlwind. As much as I wanted to control the arrangements or better yet, hire an expensive wedding planner, I used every ounce of my computer manager facade to be as gracious as possible. Many nights I came home exhausted like I had spent the day answering computer questions. Amazingly, Dennis was one of the groomsmen. Machi explained that they were treating him as innocent until proven guilty and they were praying for him.

The wedding day arrived way too soon. The other two brides maids and I went through all the traditional rituals. Machi was more excited than nervous and blushed as they made jokes about her wedding night.

"Do you know what to do, Girl?" one of her friends challenged.

"I'm aware of the parts," Machi answered laughing with beet-red face. "Not sure how to put them together."

The girls squealed with delight and whispered some advice. Seeing they were being a little too risqué, I suggested that we needed some champaign for a toast. By the time they got back and we made a toast, it was time to go to the sanctuary.

Weddings are a day of hope, yes? Two people joining together on their own journey. Most faces in the congregation were smiling and focused on the ceremony. Even Dennis seemed to be interested. The pastor spoke before saying the vows.

"The Bible refers to us, the Church, as Jesus' bride,[1]" the pastor began. "That means he loves us, he cares for us, he works for us, he gave everything for us. And he is returning soon so we can be with him."

The congregation reacted with 'amen' and applause. He, Machi and Dean then went through the vows and the pastor pronounced them 'man' and 'wife'.

"What therefore God hath joined together, let not man put asunder,[2]" the pastor finished.

We filed out of the sanctuary as we had rehearsed and got into waiting cars to be taken to the party house. Again, all the traditional rituals were followed. I used all my tricks to avoid dancing with anyone, including Dean and especially Dennis. He danced with Machi and all the bridesmaids and they seemed to enjoy his company. Obviously, they didn't know what I knew.

Pastor and Mrs. Blake made rounds, greeting everyone. A pleasant couple, who made conversation easily, they had great respect for Machi and Dean and made sure I knew I was welcome to church.

I was relieved when Machi and Dean finally decided to leave and impatient for the cab ride to be over so I could rest in my own home. As the cab pulled out of my drive, it revealed a truck that had pulled in; Dennis got out.

"Jane," he cooed, obviously drunk. "We didn't get to dance; let's dance."

My door was a few steps away. Calmly turning from him like he wasn't there, I pulled out my phone and told it to call 911. It wasn't connecting. Thinking it would connect inside, I put the key in the lock and Dennis grabbed my shoulders, turned me around and, wrapping his arm around my back, pressed me to his chest.

"I said, 'let's dance', Jane," he hissed.

It was obvious to me that he wasn't here to dance.

"You're going to jail this time, Dennis," I blurted defiantly.

He slammed me against the door making the doorknob dig into my back and I winced.

"Aw, did that hurt?" he mocked. "We can make that feel better."

He leaned close to my face and I turned away. With his free hand cupping my chin, he forced me to look at him and he brushed his lips on mine for several seconds. He pulled my hand down to caress his crotch; he was trembling.

"See there," he whispered breathlessly. "Not every man has an instrument as fine as this."

He got the door open and pushed me inside; I fell backwards sliding into a kitchen chair. As he approached me, I swung the chair at him as hard as I could, ran into a bathroom and locked the door. He was soon kicking it as I struggled to open the window. Just as he burst through the door, I plunged through the screen, wincing in pain as it scraped my arms. He grabbed my thighs but I kicked as hard as I could. My heels had to be digging into his flesh; I thought I might have hit his face because he cried loudly and bellowed curses. He let go and I fell through the window, rolling down a small hill. The nearest house was a hundred yards away. Screaming for help as loud as I could, I ran but he was faster. He tackled me. I landed on my stomach in the wet grass and he was on top of me. He turned me over, hit me hard with the palm of his hand then the back of his hand which made me cry out in pain. Then he put his hand on my throat, choking me. Keeping his hand on my throat, I heard his zipper and the sky started closing in on me; I knew I was fainting.

"God," I whispered, tears streaming. "Don't let him take my gift."

"Oh, Honey" Dennis murmured, "Your gift is coming."

"Please God," I begged as everything went gray.

He let go of my throat and, gasping for breath, I tried to turn over. My vision was blurred. Flinging my dress in my face, he put his body on top of mine. His fine instrument was touching my private place; he was looking down and cursing. He spread one of my legs then the other. I tried to close them but he put his thighs under mine. He got his instrument closer and was pushing it, trying to get inside me. He stopped.

"Are you a virgin, Little Girl?" he marveled. "I never seen such a tight..."

A dog barked; then another. Dennis looked up, stared into the blackness and spewed vulgarities; then he shot up and ran off, cursing.

"Boys!" a man yelled at his dogs then he shined a light on me. "Hey! What's going on!"

The dogs were sniffing me as I sobbed with relief, laughing at the same time. The man bent down when I didn't get up.

"Call 911," I stammered between sobs.

He started to pull my dress down to cover me, and I screamed at him not to touch me. In minutes, sirens could be heard and a squad with a police car turned into the yard. A police officer bending over me also started to pull my dress down to cover me.

"Don't move anything until you take my picture," I cried and he pulled out his phone.

Telling them the struggle began at the back door, more police cars arrived. I advised them that he probably had marks on his chest where I kicked him and I may have kicked his face. They went into my house and I prayed they were taking pictures. The officer took statements from the man with the dogs. In the emergency room, they took pictures of the bruises on my face and neck and the long scratches on my arms from the screen. They bagged my dress; they scraped under my nails and put the debris in a bottle; they swabbed my lips and between my legs. With a disposable cloth, they wiped every place he touched me and the cloth was put into an evidence bag. As these well-meaning strangers violated my body, I prayed all this would get Dennis convicted. I promised Dennis he was going to jail, and I meant it! A police officer stopped by to tell me that Dennis was apprehended and, when he could not explain the wound on his face or verify his whereabouts between the time he was last seen and when 911 was called, he asked for a lawyer. They arrested him. The officer added that my heel had stabbed him in an eye and they were getting a search warrant to swab and wipe his body. Though his eye was getting medical attention, he had to stay in his cell until the search warrant was approved or denied.

After several hours, they were going to release me but my only clothes was a bra and panties so someone offered me a scrub shirt and pants. Seeing myself in the scrub outfit and white heels made me laugh and everyone joined me. A police officer offered to take me home; she had my keys, phone and purse. Not wanting to go into the house, she was kind enough to take me to the Gladstone Hotel. I had no explanation to offer the hotel personnel for the scrub outfit; not something you can blame on an airline.

In my room, I sat on the balcony and looked at the cloudless night sky. It occurred to me that, on the night Machi was welcoming Dean's instrument into her private place, I was fighting off Dennis' invasion of mine. The same private parts; two scenarios. Machi's scenario was blessed by God and leading to happiness; I had no idea where I was headed. As though my body could no longer hold it back, sorrow broke out in deep sobs. Dropping to my knees, I then lay flat on the floor. In the midst of the sobbing and moaning, I fell asleep.

The next morning, my phone rang; it was Machi.

"Jane!" Machi blurted. "Are you alright? Dean said Dennis is in jail. Are you alright?"

More tears escaped.

"I'm a little shaken, of course," I replied, "but I'll be alright."

"Dean said you poked Dennis' eye out!" Machi exclaimed. "What did he do?"

"He tried to rape me," I answered flatly. "God rescued me though."

"God rescued you?" Machi yelled. "Praise God!"

She turned from the phone and repeated that God had rescued me.

"I told Dean that God rescued you," Machi explained.

She made me laugh. She wanted to know more and I provided highlights of the event; she didn't need the gruesome details and I didn't want to say them.

"God sent the dogs?" Machi roared laughing then she repeated it to Dean.

Chapter 10

Once again running from a house that had been violated, I remained at the Gladstone, stuck there until Dennis' trial. With no-one around to complain about the extravagance, I signed a six-month contract on the penthouse. Martin was using the Victorian as a showplace for his work; unfortunately he couldn't afford to buy it and he didn't want me to sell it.

Machi, still going to school, visited regularly. She and Dean bought a large farm and Dean was managing it. They of course wanted me to build a house on their property but I planned to get away as soon as Dennis was in jail.

BT visited to notify me that Dennis' lawyer asked for a plea bargain: Dennis would plead guilty for two years in jail.

"NO WAY!" I cried shooting out of my chair.

"But..." BT began.

"FORGET IT!" I bellowed pacing in front of him then I stopped and pointed a finger at him. "YOU would agree with me if you had been his victim!"

I paced more.

"In fact, YOU would agree with me if you had even *witnessed* what he did," I added then it occurred to me.

"You never found Jill's phone, did you?" I guessed.

"No," he answered weakly then he pleaded. "We tried, Jane, I promise..."

"I can find that video," I seethed.

He shook his head. I was infuriated.

"Are you going to set this monster free to rape someone else?" I raged.

BT walked to the door, glanced at me then left. With adrenaline pumping, I continued to pace. Looking to Heaven, I repeated that I could find that video.

In a few days, Jeff, Jill's father, visited me with a laptop bag.

"I was sorry to hear about..." he started.

"Thank you," I interrupted, not wanting him to describe the incident.

He looked down as his face puckered to hold back tears.

"You'd think after nearly three years, I could think about her without weeping," he continued then looked away from me. "We were planning her wedding...she was so happy."

Tears of sympathy wet my face.

"Dean called and said you wanted to look for the video," he stated as he handed the laptop bag to me. "I've been asking God for peace; you might be his answer."

Taking it, I asked if he knew the password and he didn't but he stayed with me as I turned on the laptop. He had her email which worked as her logon. For the password, I had a list of universal codes my father had given me. These are codes computer manufacturers built into the computer for situations like this. None of them worked. Jeff suggested Dean, variations of Dean, DeanCliff then JillCliff, which would have been her married name. It worked. Both of us cheered and I ordered lunch.

The next task was finding the backup site for her phone. Her email account contained subscription confirmations from the backup company. Opening the backup website, a notice popped up that the subscription had been cancelled due to non-payment. Jeff gave me a credit card number to reinstate the account and, we held our breath hoping Jill's files were intact. They were! Finding a document listing her passwords, we stared with anticipation and dread at her calendar, her contacts and her photos.

Jeff and I practically stopped breathing as we opened the file folder with videos and there were several, sorted by date. Scrolling to the bottom, we saw a video posted on the night she died. We didn't open it. Neither of us wanted to see it. I called BT. He said to call the police.

The officer who answered our call was the female officer, Dot, who had so kindly brought me to the Gladstone. She asked where the laptop came from and how we got into the folder. She wanted to play the video and we told her we didn't want to see it. Dot took a picture of the laptop and the bag and emailed it to us with a receipt. She said she would call when she could. Jeff left with her.

In a few hours, Dot called. The video was sufficient evidence to press charges for the attempted rape of Jill Hilledebrand. I shouted with joy and, as I had seen Machi do, I praised God.

When I next saw BT, he again wanted me to accept a plea deal; still only 4 years.

"Did you see Jill's video?" I wailed. "Go for the maximum sentence! What is wrong with you?"

"He might get off if we go to trial," BT explained.

"How can that be possible?" I bellowed. "His DNA and hair was on me; my DNA and hair was on him; his eye is destroyed!"

BT didn't speak. Then it dawned on me.

"It's money, isn't it?" I accused. "The county doesn't want to spend the money on a 'minor' case like this."

BT didn't answer.

"It's because of money that you didn't find Jill's video, isn't it?" I challenged then, with horror, I had a realization. "Finding that video was amazingly easy."

Pacing in front of BT like an enraged prosecutor interrogating a serial killer, I stopped with my hands on my hips, as close to him as I could be without touching him.

"She was dead so you didn't search for the video. Right?" I seethed.

BT sighed and shifted.

"Here is a message for Mr. Dennis Cliff," I hissed, bending, putting my hands on the arms of BT's chair, so close to his face, I could feel his breath. "I want a trial with maximum penalty and, IF he 'gets off' or IF his sentence is less than maximum penalty, I will sue him on my behalf and THEN, I will sue him on Jill's behalf."

Staring at BT daring him to protest, I continued.

"Do you understand me?" I demanded.

BT rose, making me step back and walked to the door.

"I hear you," he said.

On the day of Dennis' sentence hearing, I was eager to leave my sanctuary because I wanted to see him vanquished. I wanted to see his miserable head hanging down in sorrow and, hopefully, fear. I wanted his jail to be the most vile jail on the earth. Seated in the back of the courtroom, I watched Dennis shuffle to the defendants' table. He wore an eye patch. Bailey was not his lawyer. The bailiff called the court to order, announced the judge and the participants. The judge read the charges and asked Dennis for his plea. He pled guilty. I wanted to shout but I smiled and looked victoriously to Heaven. The judge then explained his perspective on the case, citing both rape attempts, and announced the sentence: 14 years in prison - the maximum. Rushing from the courtroom, I could not wait to shout for joy.

That night, as I sat on the balcony of my penthouse suite, looking for vacation packages to Italy, I thought about Dennis 14 years from now. He would be 42, a convicted felon and cutting grass his only experience. Maybe he would be homeless! Wondering if he would still want to rape, I thought maybe I should plan to monitor his whereabouts.

Then, I checked myself, thankfully. God stopped Dennis from stealing my virginity; now Dennis was stealing my life. Actually, he had stolen the last three years: he stole my job, the house and routine that I loved, my Victorian that I loved, and tens of thousands of dollars as I hid in this penthouse. Looking to God, I asked him for the answer.

As the days passed, I busied myself getting ready for a trip to Italy, Tuscany, to be exact. My parents had stayed at a luxurious hotel in a remote area of Tuscany; the 'entertainment' there was nature walks and cooking - so different from most resorts. My passport had to be replaced; I struggled to decide if I wanted to buy luggage or just buy clothes in Italy. Machi objected to my spending money on clothes so she borrowed a suitcase and helped me pack.

The plane ride was long but, in first class, it was like spending the day in a friend's living room. In the airport, I stopped at a coffee shop, called the hotel to send a car and waited for them to text me. To my amazement, I saw Brad walking toward me. He sat down without asking my permission.

"What..." I started.

"What am I doing here?" he interrupted. "I'm collecting a bounty."

"You're a bounty hunter?" I exclaimed then laughed involuntarily. "Why?"

"Why am I working, you mean?" Brad elaborated. "Why am I not living in luxury like you are?"

He looked away, scowling.

"My mother is still living," Brad continued. "She lives like there is no money and she expects the same of me."

I nodded with understanding, knowing Ronald would live that way.

"Isn't piloting a good income?" I wondered.

"Yeah, if you can stand people," he seethed. "Stupid, ignorant people."

Wincing, I realized that his perspective of people, though more hateful, was similar to mine.

"It's quite a coincidence that your victim is in this part of the world," I observed.

Brad looked at me with disdain.

"Really?" he mocked, the same way he did at our first meeting.

My eyes widened.

"It's me?" I stammered.

He nodded.

"You said I was safe!" I blurted.

"You were safe," he answered, "in America."

"Isn't the bounty on my father? On Ronald?" I cried, starting to panic.

Brad chuckled seeming to enjoy my reaction.

"Your stupid pictures were published worldwide," he hissed.

"Stupid pictures?" I repeated, not knowing what he meant.

"You're zillion dollar home in your zillion dollar outfits and jewels," he explained then he leaned toward me. "You used your real name, Nitwit."

As though Brad had hit me, I shot back in my chair.

"They want the money," he answered. "With interest"

"Who is 'they'!" I demanded.

"The men your father talked about," Brad described sardonically. "The men my father was hiding from. We spent our entire life hiding, watching, waiting..."

Brad looked away like he was remembering. I remember, too, the precautions my father took: never establish a routine, never engage strangers, never reveal plans, keep moving, make reservations at the very last minute, and so on.

"Tell them I'll meet with them," I suggested. "We can work this out."

Brad, laughing to himself, looked at the crowd of people walking past the coffee shop.

"You don't get it!" he stated finally. "Your father and my father weren't the thieves; they were the victims. These men are the thieves! They are mobsters!"

"How do you know these men!" I cried. "Why aren't they after Ronald's money?"

"Look," he scowled. "I made a deal with them, OK? I told them, when my mother dies, I'll give them the money. They agreed to let her live her life."

"And that's it? Just like that you have a deal with Mobsters?" I challenged. "You should work for the State Department."

Brad's phone rang and he turned away from me. When he ended the call, he bent down close to my ear.

"Ok," he whispered fiercely. "I'm working for the mobsters. It's work for them or die. Alright?"

He stood up then bent down again.

"And both of us are running out of time," he continued. "Come with me quietly; I'll make the best deal for you that I can. They are getting impatient."

Sighing deeply, I looked to Heaven and closed my eyes. Jill's statement, 'God is real', came to my mind as well as the barking dogs chasing Dennis away.

"Are you coming?" Brad pressed.

"No," I answered, getting up. "I'm going home."

Following me to the information center, Brad loosed a barrage of vulgarities then grasped my arm so tightly, it made me wince in pain.

"If I walk away from here with no money, they will come for you," Brad announced. "They will make you pay it off as a sex slave. If you're lucky, you'll get a master who isn't a sadist."

Having just been assaulted by a sadist; having seen news reports, read romance novels and seen horror movies about sadists, I had visions of what that would mean. Brad seemed to know what I was thinking.

"They know where Machi is, Jane," Brad stated. "They know where she goes to school."

Finally taking a few seconds to study Brad, I saw fear in his eyes. Though he was trying to scare me, he was actually pleading for his life.

"What are you going to do?" he asked with a sigh, looking around.

"I'm giving this situation to God," I declared as I resumed walking to the Information Center. "I suggest you do the same."

"Are you out of your mind?" Brad bellowed as he trailed behind me. "Give it to 'God'?"

He put 'God' in air quotes. Then he laughed.

"God is not *here!*" he declared, "Therefore, I *can't* 'give it to 'God' ."

He laughed again as though my suggestion was absurd.

"Give it to me, then!" I bellowed back.

Stopping so quickly he almost ran into me, I turned to face him.

"I'm not the one who needs rescued," I exclaimed. "Come home with me."

His face immediately softened, his eyes widened and, though he was staring at me, he seemed to be envisioning something else. His freedom, perhaps.

"You need to disappear," I continued. "Drop off the radar. You need to walk away from the money, from..."

"I know what to do," Brad said quietly, factually. "My mother...."

"Bring her," I answered.

"Can we sit down?" Brad asked.

I followed him to a secluded spot.

"We have to buy some time," Brad began, "and the only way to buy time is to tell the mobsters that you have to liquidate assets. They are going to know how much time you need. I'll tell them I will keep you in a hotel room until the transfer is made."

This meant I had to trust Brad! Fear pierced my heart then I decided to follow my own suggestion: 'Let God handle it'.

Brad made the call. They gave him three days.

"Do you have cash?" Brad asked.

"I have fifteen hundred dollars," I answered.

"Excellent!", he smiled, a cute, sincere smile.

"You have to ditch your phone and laptop," he stated.

"Oh!" I gasped, though I knew he was right.

Looking at my phone, I had a text from the resort car. I texted that I was going to be delayed. Then, backing up my phone and laptop, I disabled both of them then I disabled Brad's phone.

"Now, we leave the airport to give the impression we are going to a hotel," Brad explained. "Then we'll hitch a ride on a private jet."

"You do have an escape plan," I declared.

"I do, Jane," Brad responded. "I certainly do."

Arriving at a private jet facility, Brad led me to a chair and said he would return. Though I couldn't hear the words, Brad was talking to someone and there was some laughing. When he returned to me, he said we had to wait for a flight to come in and we had to wait a long time. Finally, we were allowed to board and we were escorted to the crew's quarters. Brad thankfully found some soda and snacks.

Brad explained that he made many friends in the airline industry and it was common, though not legal maybe, for fellow pilots to allow friends on flights. It was his job as a pilot that brought him in contact with the mobsters who lured him with money to be their pilot. When they discovered Ronald's wealth and realized Brad's mother had control of it, Brad made the deal with them: They agreed to let Brad's mother live if Brad would do their bidding and turn over the money when he got control of it.

When we landed in the United States, we found another flight to get to Brad's mother. Buying a junk car with half of the cash, we got to her house, which was actually a trailer. Brad would not let me out of the car. He rushed into the trailer and I could hear him shouting at her. Finally she appeared at the door of the trailer walking briskly to the car, looking as though she were running from a fire. Brad practically pushed her into the car as she turned to protest. She was terrified and sobbing grasping a small Bible and some rosary beads. Before Brad could take off, I got in the back seat to console her.

"You're going to be alright," I began, taking her hand. "My name is Jane."

She was fragile and thin, silver hair, thick glasses and didn't say anything.

"Jane, this is my mother, Martha," Brad stated, looking at us in the rear view mirror.

"You can stay with me, now, OK, Martha?" I suggested.

She looked at me with question and didn't answer. I didn't try to convince her she would be alright. Brad drove to a private jet facility and again, we had to wait over 24 hours for a flight that could take us close to the farm. We bought a prepaid phone and I called Machi.

"You're on a prepaid phone," she cried. "What's wrong! I've been trying to call you!"

I explained what happened.

"I have to get Dean," Machi wailed. "He's in the field and I have to ride to him."

A door slammed and a motor started. It sounded like an ATV[3]. After a few minutes, Machi said she could see him. The motor stopped and Machi was breathless when she put the phone on speaker, repeating the situation.

"Where are you?" Dean asked. "We can buy airline tickets..."

"We don't have identification," I explained. "We had to go underground. I left everything in Italy. But Brad can get us to...where? Brad?"

Brad took the phone and explained to Dean how they could get close to the farm. Brad said he would call as soon as we landed. Dean said he would pick us up.

Seeing Machi and Dean's car in line at the airport to pick us up, was as exciting as waiting in line to see Santa. Rushing toward her, she saw me and waved. We reached for each other to embrace. Brad and Martha walked up behind me and it was a happy reunion for Machi and Martha. Immediately, Martha talked about the day that Machi 'disappeared' and no-one would explain. Machi directed Martha into the back seat and Machi sat with her. When Martha complained that Brad made her leave everything including her trailer, Machi suggested that a trailer could be installed next to the house. I added, for Brad's sake, that a house could eventually be built for them. Looking at Dean for approval, he nodded in agreement.

It was a long ride home and all of us were exhausted when we pulled into the farm. Machi brought a pillow and blankets for Brad to sleep on the couch. Martha was taken to the guest bedroom and Machi directed me to another small bedroom. Their house was clean and pleasant but it was old; not updated, which was Ronald's influence. Before laying down, I knelt and thanked God for rescuing me again.

Chapter 11

The next morning, I woke and found myself waiting for a turn in their one bathroom, amazed that Machi had a zillion dollars and didn't spend it on upgrades. Peaking out of the door, occasionally, Brad emerged then I rushed in. Though I wanted to shower, I assumed other people would be waiting for a turn so I washed a little and used the deodorant in the cabinet. When I got downstairs, Machi was serving coffee and breakfast. She said she didn't need any help so I got coffee and toast. Brad was quiet. I asked about Martha and Machi said she was still sleeping.

"She sleeps a lot these days," Brad offered.

"How old is she?" I asked.

He had to think about it.

"She'll be 67 this year," he figured. "Stress has worn her down, I think."

Knowing Brad had nothing, I wasn't sure how open he was to help but I decided to find out.

"You and Martha need clothes and things," I began. "I can make you a family member on a credit card."

I will never forget how he looked at me in response.

"Thank you," he said simply but deeply. "For the first time in my life, I'm free."

"That's what Ronald said," I remembered.

"Exactly," Brad responded. "He had to die to be free. I...I..."

Looking away and sighing deeply, he continued.

"This is miraculous," he stated, looking at Heaven. "Miraculous."

He continued to look to Heaven and I didn't want to interrupt his thoughts.

"You can build a house here," I finally offered. "How 'bout a cabin in the woods?"

He laughed.

"I'll take the dog house, at this point," he replied with his cute smile.

"We can install a trailer for Martha," Machi added, "and Francisco Farms hires crop dusters."

"I'd need a license for that," Brad reminded her.

"You can get a new identity," Machi suggested.

Brad nodded in agreement.

"I can give you BT's number," I offered. "He's a lawyer. But we need to get you a phone first, I guess."

When Martha came down and had breakfast, Machi took us to town for phones, laptops, clothes, a trailer. Martha was thrilled to be able to pick the trailer that she wanted. I think she was thrilled to have so much attention showered on her. Then they left me at my penthouse suite. I had a month left on the lease and now a bedroom would be available at Machi's house for Brad.

The next morning, I was glad when Machi invited me to come look for a place to build my house. Dean had two ATV's[4] waiting, one for Dean and Machi and the other for Brad and me. He led us down a line of trees and stopped to show us places where he would build a house. Then he went into the woods, crossed a small stream and talked about sites that he liked. As we headed out of the woods, Dean toured his fields and stopped to explain what was being planted and some of his future plans. Then I think we went on some joy-riding as Dean increased speed and Brad kept up with him. Brad looked like a completely different person as he enjoyed the ride, the speed, the fresh air and sunshine.

The next week, I asked Martin, the interior designer, if he would review the land and pick a spot for a house. Brad agreed to let Martin review the sites in the woods for his cabin. On the ATV's Martin rode with me and we followed Brad. To Martin's dismay, Brad and I also engaged in a little joy-riding as Brad sped up and I tried to keep up. Brad was more reckless than me, though. Over the following months, the three of us met often reviewing architectural plans and everything else associated with a house: flooring, lighting, tile, landscaping, siding, paint and so on. Sometimes, during these sessions, we would glance at each other and, wondering if he wanted to ask me out, I avoided being alone with him.

Allison, my former supervisor, called one day, just checking in, she said, and invited me to have chili with them again. I suggested that it was my turn to host and she agreed to come to the farm. We decided to cook over a campfire. Martha joined us for a little while then said she preferred to be inside. Allison, Machi, Alex and Dean, being born-again, talked freely and happily about God, Jesus, the Bible and the Holy Spirit, which I had yet to hear about. When I mentioned that, someone said that I sounded like the disciples in Ephesus[5].

"Actually," I stated with a half-smile, "I don't know what you mean by 'born-again.'"

The four of them looked at each other, not knowing who should respond. Machi spoke. Brad listened quietly.

"God made Adam from dust, right?" she began. "That was his first birth."

She looked at me and I nodded that I understood.

"Then God breathed *life* into Adam," Machi explained. "In other words, God's *spirit* went into Adam.[6] That was his second birth."

She looked at me and, again, I nodded.

"So, God has to breathe life into our spirits as well, right?" Machi continued. "Until he does that, we have the life of the flesh but we don't have the life of the spirit.[7]"

"Okay," I said. "That makes sense. Why doesn't God breathe life into everyone?"

"God wants us to *choose* him," Dean answered, "and he wants us to *commit* to him."

"The Bible says in many places that, if we believe in Jesus, we will be saved or born-again," Machi answered. "But..."

She looked at me seriously.

"But 'believing' is not like believing in Santa," she smiled. "We have to 'believe' in him like we would believe in someone we want to marry. We have to 'trust' him, we have to 'want' him..."

"We have to 'like' him, Allison added.

" 'Follow' him," Dean added.

"Yes," Machi agreed. "Following him means reading the Bible, understanding his teachings and making them the principles of your life. The Bible calls this 'repenting'. Do you want to follow Jesus?"

"I do," I said immediately, as warm tears flowed softly.

"OKAY!" she beamed smiling broadly as she jumped up and rushed to hug me.

"And the Holy Spirit?" I pressed.

"Oh!" Machi exclaimed. "As Jesus told his disciples that the Holy Spirit will guide them[8], that same Holy Spirit will guide us and help us follow Jesus."

I looked at Brad.

"I'm born-again," I declared, smiling.

Brad got up and walked toward the house; I followed him.

"What's wrong?" I asked.

When he was several feet away from the campfire, he stopped to answer me.

"I'm not religious," Brad began. "I don't want to be religious. My mother forced me to..."

"Nobody's making you be religious," I retorted.

"I feel pressured to be," Brad exclaimed. "Dean praises God all day long and now you are 'born-again'."

"You said being here is 'miraculous', didn't you?" I reminded him. "Weren't you referring to something God did?"

"It did feel like a miracle," Brad agreed. "Am I now required to become a priest?"

"No, nothing like that," I insisted. "Please believe me. No-one wants to 'enslave' you. All of us want you to have peace and joy."

I looked at Machi, Allison, Dean and Alex all laughing at something.

"They want the best for you," I continued. "To them, Jesus is the best they can give."

Having nothing else to say, Brad turned toward the house.

"Have you called BT?" I asked.

Brad stopped and shook his head that he hadn't.

"Why don't you call him?" I suggested. "It might help if you can get a new identity established and start doing something you like to do."

"Good idea," he muttered as he disappeared into the house.

Church and Bible study became important parts of my routine. As BT said it would, reading the Bible and praying made God real to me. I came to know him as the owner of everything made, including me. As his love for me became real, sin in me also became real. Once I understood the reality of sin and God's hatred of it, I realized what Jesus did for me. I came to cherish his forgiveness and realized I needed to forgive others in the same way.

When, Martha and Brad got moved into the trailer and the penthouse lease was up, Machi invited me to stay with them as my house got built. Watching Machi and Dean interact was amazing. Dean was in the fields or in the barns most of the time, but when he walked through the door, as my father did, he wanted to know where Machi was if she wasn't in the room. Dean always showered after he came home and Machi usually had a reason to be upstairs with him. Though Machi had the meal prepared and the table set, they cleaned up together. On the nights they were not attending a church or farm association event, they took walks or an ATV ride, or if weather was bad, they sat in their comfortable living room reading something on their devices or watching a video together. It was noticeable that they avoided secular media. Machi said they wanted everything in their home to honor God. Any issue or problem on which they did not agree was settled by quiet conversation, each presenting their opinion. Most of their opinions were based on scripture. Machi, most of the time, acquiesced to Dean, which I didn't understand. When I mentioned that she seemed to give in to him, she answered that she let the responsibility for the decision fall on him and on God. Eventually I understood this was a source of her peace.

Sunday mornings, we, including Martha, attended church and tagging along with Machi and Dean was the perfect arrangement for me. As people greeted us or stopped to engage in conversation, Machi and Dean did all the talking and I smiled or laughed when appropriate. Assuming God was aware of my social phobias, I thanked him often. It was a little harder to keep turning down the invitations to the many, many activities available at church, especially since I wasn't working and had plenty of time. Finally, I mentioned to Machi and Dean that I wanted to work. Dean said jobs were available at Francisco Farms; he had become acquainted with the Francisco family at a farmers' association meeting and gave me a contact name. Because Dean had a good opinion of the owners, I mailed my resume.

In a few days, I was waiting to speak to Francisco Farms' personnel manager and David Stone, Dean's lawyer at Dennis' trial, walked into the office.

"Jane?" David asked looking at me.

"Hello," I responded with surprise.

"Are you applying for a job?" he asked with wonder.

I nodded that I was, and the personnel manager came out of her office.

"You can't hire this person," David teased with a smile.

"I'll decide that," she quipped and led me away.

Looking at my resume, she asked the usual questions, one of them being why I quit my job and what I had been doing. Being as general as possible, I explained the events that had interrupted my life. When I left her office, David was waiting for me.

"How'd it go?" he inquired.

"I'm not sure," I answered. "She didn't hire me so I won't know until she calls me back or I get a letter of rejection."

I turned to leave.

"How have you been?" he continued with an interest I considered to be genuine but all I could think of was how he had abandoned the search for Jill's video.

Assuming he was the Francisco Farm's lawyer, I asked why he was here.

"My children work here," David explained. "Their mother was one of the daughters of the Francisco Farms' founder."

"Then, they are in management, yes?" I guessed.

"Right, they are," he affirmed, "but we made them start at the bottom, including shoveling manure."

He laughed and looked off as though he was remembering those days.

"Losing your wife must have been tough," I ventured.

He sighed deeply and looked to Heaven.

"Nothing in my life has been harder," David murmured. "Your case was tough, though."

"You got that right," I agreed. "Got a time machine handy? I want a redo."

David laughed and studied me for a minute.

"Maybe we can have dinner," he suggested with a smile.

Stiffening, I backed away from him.

"I..I can't right now," I stuttered and turned to leave, not wanting to see his expression.

Chapter 12

One Sunday, we were seated, waiting for the service to start and Machi pointed to someone and said something to Dean. Looking in the direction where she pointed, a tall, heavy, bearded man with shoulder-length hair, somewhat familiar, walked into the sanctuary. He was with a few other men, followed by a police officer.

"Do you know him?" I asked Machi.

"It's Dennis," Machi answered flatly, not looking at me.

I gasped. This man was at least a hundred pounds heavier than Dennis was, years ago, and he looked older than his actual age.

"What..." I blurted.

"He has been allowed to attend service," Machi explained.

"Why didn't you tell me?" I demanded, getting angry, feeling betrayed.

Standing up to leave, Dennis glanced my way.

"Oh, great!" I uttered.

Machi gently took hold of my arm, trying to pull me down. I gave in to her.

"He can't hurt you," Machi assured me. "He can't hurt anyone. He's under guard."

Though I realized she was right, I still wanted to leave. His presence replayed that night in my mind including emotions.

"I don't care," I cried. "I'm leaving."

"Where are you going?" Machi asked with concern.

"I'll go to the airport and wait for my flight," I answered.

When the congregation stood to sing, I shuffled past Machi and Dean and walked outside. Calling a cab, I went to the airport and looked for a flight to my destination that was leaving sooner. Although I found one, it was still an hour wait. Walking toward the gate, I stopped at the coffee shop. Once I got seated, I started to tremble and wanted so much to cry.

"Dear God," I whispered. "Will I ever be 'normal'? Will I ever be like Machi and Dean, in a loving, secure relationship? Will I ever stop being afraid?"

My phone rang; it was Machi.

"Where are you?" Machi asked, sounding worried.

"I'm at the airport," I answered. "My flight leaves in 30 minutes."

"I have your laptop and bag," Machi stated. "What gate?"

Letting out an involuntary laugh, I told her the gate number.

"I'm walking there now," Machi responded.

Eating my food and drink on the way, I reached the gate and saw Machi as soon as I turned to look. She smiled at me and waved. Rushing to her, I wrapped my arms around her then took my things.

"You are so precious," I whispered. "Thank you."

"I knew you would have to spend money on clothes and a toothbrush," she laughed, which made me laugh.

"I wish I could take you with me," I said. "Maybe we could have a girls' weekend."

"That's a great idea!" Machi agreed. "But listen..."

She walked to a chair and gently pulled me along.

"You need to know something about Dennis," Machi began.

I stiffened not wanting to hear but decided to let her talk.

"He's taking medicine," she continued. "It makes him sexless."

"Sexless?" I blurted.

"Yes," Machi affirmed then whispered. "He doesn't want sex."

"How..." I started.

"They offered it to him and he agreed," Machi interrupted. "He's like a eunuch, in the Bible."

Airline representatives started boarding the plane.

"Did they cut it off?" I marveled, referring to his 'fine instrument'.

Machi leaned back laughing.

"No, no," she replied. "It doesn't work when he takes the medicine."

The airline representative announced my class and I got up.

"I'll call you," I stated and walked to get in line.

"Wait!" Machi cried. "I was going to tell you at dinner today, I'm pregnant!"

I squealed with delight, clapping and she joined me. With a quick hug, I rushed to board the plane.

The next Saturday night, just as we were getting ready to clean up from supper, Dean got a call and he took it on the porch. It was Dennis; Dean had him on speaker. Dennis was objecting to attending church.

"God has everything you need," Dean advised.

"I can't live that life," Dennis complained. "I'm not like you. I can't memorize scripture, pray for hours, *tithe...*"

Dennis sighed loudly.

"Dennis!" Dean blurted as though demanding his attention. "I've told you, those things aren't *required.*"

"That's not what the preachers here say," Dennis insisted. "Being a Christian is like having a full time job that you hate. I'm being honest with you. I can't do it."

"It's your decision, of course," Dean said sadly. "But you're cheating yourself. God is amazing."

Dennis didn't respond.

"Okay," Dean concluded. "I'll visit you tomorrow."

Dean returned to the kitchen and took his place beside Machi who was at the sink rinsing dishes. She put his arm on his waist to hug him. He bent down and kissed the top of her head.

"We could hear you," I offered.

Dean looked at me.

"Oh, no problem," he said.

"Why does Dennis think that being a Christian is work?" I asked. "Brad thinks the same thing."

"A lot of people think that, I'm sad to say," Dennis answered. "We are fortunate that Pastor Blake is able to explain the difference between 'faith' and 'works.'"

I remembered the pastor teaching about works. He said that, when we are born-again, we enter into God's 'rest'[9] and, because we love God and with the help of the Holy Spirit, we live lives that please God. Reading the Bible and praying pleases God, loving our neighbor pleases God, and so on. Just like I had to do things for my earthly father who I loved, I do these things for my heavenly father who I love. Wanting so much for Brad to understand, it was surprising to me that I also wished Dennis would understand.

Walking onto the porch to enjoy the sunset and the cool evening air, Brad was approaching the trailer in an ATV. He saw me and stopped in front of the porch.

"Your house looks like it's ready," Brad offered. "The cabin is ready."

"Wonderful," I responded. "I'll check it out tomorrow. I'm surprised Martin hasn't called."

"He was here a few days ago," Brad answered. "He's been really busy."

Brad got off the ATV and sat on the porch steps, looking up at me.

"I told him to get whatever furniture he wanted for the cabin, OK?" Brad stated.

"Yes, of course," I agreed. "I love his work."

"It's been almost a year since the 'great escape,'" he said thoughtfully. "Maybe we should celebrate."

Thinking this moment would come and dreading it, I deflected.

"You realize now, of course, that the gowns and jewels in that magazine weren't mine," I challenged.

"Magazine?" Brad questioned but then seemed to remember immediately. "Oh, the magazine! Yes, I realize that now."

Brad looked away toward the sunset.

"I never apologized for berating you," Brad stated, getting up, obviously getting the hint. "I know now you are not a 'nitwit' and I'm sorry if I hurt you."

Brad kept his distance after that night and I wondered if I had made a mistake. When he moved into his cabin, I rarely saw him. When I moved into my house, it was clear that Brad's cabin had become a social gathering place for the farm hands. Dean said they drank and played poker; watched sports. He felt sure all of it was harmless. One Friday night, having returned home from weekly travels, I was sitting on my deck feeling jet lag and Brad rode by on an ATV with a woman passenger. Sighing deeply, I looked to Heaven and prayed for him to be born-again. Then, feeling a pang of loneliness, I prayed for God's will to be done in me, wondering if his will included a relationship like Machi and Dean's.

Chapter 13

Machi brought home her baby girl, Kalani Jane. 'Kalani', after her mother and 'Jane' after me; she was so delicate and beautiful. Taking some vacation, I stayed home with them while Dean went to the fields. Every morning, Machi and Dean read the Bible together, talked a little about its meaning and prayed. In addition, Dean was gone every day at lunch, visiting Dennis. Dennis had stopped coming to church and, as I prayed for Brad to be born-again, I found myself praying for Dennis also.

On one of my trips, I called Machi one night and asked her if I could talk to Dennis, let him know that I forgive him and invite him to church. She turned away from the phone, said something to Dean, then came back and said that Dennis would call but it would be a collect call. The next night, my phone rang and I was asked to accept a collect call.

"Dennis?" I asked softly.

"Yeah, who's this?" he said with suspicion.

"This is Jane Fortner," I answered.

There was silence for several seconds.

"Dennis?" I repeated.

"Yeah," he said reluctantly almost whispering.

"I wanted to invite you to church," I began.

"Why?" he grunted.

"It will help you," I stated. "It's a good thing. Also I wanted you to know that I for..."

"I'm here because of *you,*" he blurted.

Suddenly the desire to kill rose in me. I looked to Heaven and asked God to help me. Taking a deep breath, I continued.

"You put yourself there, Dennis, and you know that," I retorted firmly yet without anger.

"Fourteen years!" he bellowed. "Fourteen years in this hell-hole! The best years of my life!"

He slammed the phone ending the call. This was so different than I thought it would be! In my imagination, I thought he would accept my invitation, shave his beard, cut his hair, loose a hundred pounds and come to church. So different! It never occurred to me that *he* would have to forgive *me*! Thinking back on that day in court when I rejoiced at his sentence, I realized how much hate I was spewing. I didn't know it then, but God viewed my behavior toward Dennis as sinful as what Dennis had done to me. Both behaviors despicable to God and both worthy of sentence to hell. Looking to Heaven, I thanked God for loving me anyway, for letting Jesus bear the wrath I deserved, and I prayed sincerely for Dennis to be born-again.

My travels that week ended on a Thursday because of a corporate meeting. As I walked out of the meeting room, someone said my name. It was David Stone and he quipped that we would have to stop meeting like this. He asked how things were going and I told him about Machi's baby; we talked for quite a while. At the end, he again invited me to dinner. Complimenting him on his tenacity, I accepted. The smile on his face was rewarding.

On the night of our date, David picked me up in a luxurious red sports car instead of his truck. Dean, coming from the barn, nodded to David as he passed the car. We did not go to a Francisco Farms Restaurant. David, instead, took me to the same five-star hotel where I had drenched those unfortunate patrons. It happened to be a country club where David played golf.

"I owe you an apology," I announced after we ordered our meal.

"Really?" David answered with surprise.

"I accused you of not pursuing Jill's video because she was dead," I explained.

David sighed.

"BT told me how upset you were," he relayed. "And why wouldn't you be angry? We wouldn't expect any other reaction."

"I need to apologize to BT, too," I continued. "He looked like a whipped puppy when he left my hotel room."

We both laughed.

"Please don't worry about it," David begged. "Lawyers have thick skin. We work in an atmosphere of emotion, mostly unhappiness. We have to distance ourselves from it."

The food arrived.

"I found a world of peace," I offered.

"That sounds wonderful," David marveled. "Take me to your leader."

"The leader is Jesus," I answered, smiling.

"Oh," David responded nodding, choking a little on his drink. "I see."

"We attend the college church, if you'd like to go," I suggested. "The pastor is exceptional."

"Thank you," David said politely. "I know that church."

David changed the conversation to BT's growing family then, when we were done eating, he took me home. When I got out of David's car, I stopped in to say 'good night' to Machi and Dean. Machi, sitting on the couch with Dean, expressed surprise that I was home so early. Dean snickered.

"You had dinner at a hotel, right?" he guessed.

"Yes," I answered with wonder.

"He didn't offer to get a room?" Dean guessed again.

"No!" I blurted, insulted.

"That's why she's home early," Dean said, turning to Machi.

"He was expecting me to sleep with him?" I gasped. "He never acted like that..."

"You were BT's client then," Dean explained. "Now you're fair game."

"So David equates 'dating' with 'sex'?" I sighed.

"A lot of guys do, don't they?" Dean answered, "And women foolishly go along."

"You could have warned me!" I blurted.

"Not my business," Dean stated.

"Please, next time, warn me," I begged.

Dean leaned toward me.

"Ok, then, " he began, "have a seat."

I sat down wondering what he wanted to say.

"Dennis told me about the call," Dean started with irritation. "He was very upset."

"*He* was upset?" I repeated with amazement.

"Yes," Dean affirmed. "He's having a hard time."

There were two Jane's inside me wanting to respond to this. The 'flesh' Jane wanted to yell, "Good!"; the 'Spirit-filled' Jane knew better.

"I'm sorry," the 'Spirit-filled' Jane chose to say.

My answer seemed to have an effect on Dean, as though he realized he was not choosing the 'Spirit-filled' way.

"Dennis is filled with remorse for what he did to you and to Jill," Dean explained in a softer tone.

As though struck by lightening, I realized that Dennis had caused Jill's death and yet Dean visited Dennis every day.

"You have forgiven him," I stated with wonder, my eyes widened.

"Only with God's help, believe me," Dean said leaning back, taking Machi's hand. "Only with prayer and Machi's love."

Seeing them sitting together, joined together as one[10], like the Bible said, made my heart warm. Tears were flowing down all of our faces.

"How does God do that?" I wondered. "How can he neutralize that memory?"

"For me, God first made me realize that I was born in sin[11]; that I can't escape sin," Dean began. "This is what led me to Jesus, years ago.

Then, when Jill was killed, the agony led me to prayer for her mother and father and then to prayer for Dennis."

Dean lifted up Machi's hand and kissed it.

"What 'neutralized' my anger, as you called it, was understanding that Jesus absorbed my sin and Dennis' sin, and God poured out his wrath on Jesus," Dean continued then he leaned forward. "The most amazing part is that Jesus is God in the flesh. Jesus poured out his wrath on *himself*."

I nodded my head with total understanding and awe.

"Do you ever feel anger?" I asked. "Does it ever attack you?"

"Never," he stated firmly looking at Machi. "Anger has been replaced with thanksgiving."

Moving to my knees, I asked that we pray for Dennis and for me. As we prayed, a sweet presence filled the room like I had never felt. All of us raised our hands to Heaven praising and thanking God.

On my travels the next week, having supper at a restaurant, I got a call that changed my life. It was Machi.

"Jane!" Machi blurted in a panicked voice, "Your house is burned down!"

Gasping in reaction, I choked on food I was chewing that was sucked into my throat. The choking was loud and drawing attention so I put a napkin over my mouth to muffle the noise. A waiter rushed to my table to try to help, asking if I needed the Heimlich. I waved him off. Machi, on the phone, was saying my name, asking if I was alright. Finally, the coughing stopped and I took sips of water.

"Machi," I finally said. "What happened?"

"There was a bad storm," she wailed. "The lightening and thunder were horrible! It woke us up and we saw the flames. Dean said the wind was fanning the fire. By the time the fire trucks came, the house was engulfed."

She texted a video. My house looked like a giant fire pit still smoldering. Firemen were still there drenching what was left. Years ago, by myself, I would have called Ronald. This time, I looked to Heaven with thanksgiving, knowing I could stay with Machi and knowing I had the means to rebuild. Realizing there were millions, like Brad and Dennis, who weren't aware that God is real and that he loves us, I prayed for all of them to be born-again.

When I got home Friday night, Machi took me to the guest bedroom. We both laughed that I was again without a toothbrush; she showed me the cabinet where I could get one along with toiletries. The only clothes I had was in my suitcase which meant another shopping trip. We took Martha, who had been living happily in the trailer, and Kalani. We also stopped at the Victorian, still Martin's showplace, to discuss the rebuild. My brain had no problem immediately replaying the rape. Feeling sick, I hesitated getting out of the car and Machi asked if I was alright.

"I can't go in there," I wailed staring at the back door.

Machi took my hand.

"I thought you were following Jesus," Machi challenged.

"I am," I cried. "I am following him."

"Right now, you are following Fear," Machi stated. "Now is the perfect time to pray for Dennis."

She was right and I asked God to help Dennis connect to Jesus and I added Brad. I asked God to help me forgive and forget. Machi got out of the car, pulled Kalani out of the car seat, waiting for me to walk to her. She took my hand. Martha took my other one and, together, we entered triumphantly into that house of horror.

A few weeks later was Machi's graduation day, and Family gathered to celebrate. Allison, Alex, Martha, Brad with a gorgeous date, too young for him, Dean's parents arrived and to my amazement, so did Dennis. It looked like he had gained another fifty pounds still with eye patch, beard and shoulder-length hair. Like Dean, hair on top of his head was thinning.

In addition to celebrating Machi's graduation, Dean announced that Dennis was being released from prison for good behavior.

Brad also had an announcement. He introduced his date, Sally Francisco, yes, of Francisco Farms, and he was granted a new identity, Cliff Woods. When asked about his plans with his new identity, he said he had to attend the necessary classes to get a pilot license and, he said with a smile, he had a job waiting at Francisco Farms.

When Dennis was released from prison, he came to live with and work for Dean. Because all of us were using one bathroom, Dennis, by his own accord, woke first, around 4 am, to shower and go to the fields. Machi and I both marveled that Dennis never left a mess in the bathroom. If I saw him during the day, it was from a distance. At supper, Dennis' quick wit kept all of us laughing. He came up with one-liners without thinking. We also had wonderful discussions on the Bible. Dennis was learning, and Dean was a great teacher.

One day, after visiting the progress on my home, I saw Dennis leave. Asking Machi where he was going, he said he had to report to his parole officer every day for his medicine. I knew she meant the medicine that made him sexless. That made me sad for him yet I believed it was best for him.

At supper that night, I ventured to ask Dennis if I could trim his beard and hair. He said I could if I would go to dinner with him. It was a deal. Later that week, with his beard and hair trimmed, wearing a dress jacket that was a little too tight and jeans, he looked very presentable. He helped me into his polished truck and took me to my favorite restaurant. Our conversation started with Machi and Dean then he asked me about my parents. That story took up most of the evening and with our meals finished, we left for home. As we pulled into the driveway, he said there was a reason he wanted to be alone with me.

"That night you called," he began softly, "I was planning to kill myself. It had been on my mind for months. There are men in prison who will help you do that."

"How horrible!" I gasped.

"It's not play land in there," he responded shaking his head.

He hesitated, looking away from me.

"You saved my life that night, Jane," he said sincerely. "When you - the one woman in the world who should have hated me - invited me to church, I fell on my knees begging God for help."

"But," I protested, "you were so mean to me on the phone."

"Yeah, I'm sorry," he responded looking out toward the sunset. "There was a line behind me. There was a guard on the phone. Plus, it would have put you in danger."

"What?" I blurted.

"Those men have friends on the outside who harass women," Dennis explained. "They would have extorted me for the few niceties we get in there. Some of them would have extorted me for sex."

I nodded knowing about the sexual behavior in prisons.

"Wouldn't they have sex with you anyway?" I ventured.

"You can get protection if you want it," Dennis answered. "A lot of those men are evil but a lot of them aren't."

He looked down and sighed deeply.

"A lot of rapes occur in there to the younger, weaker men," he stated sadly. "Seeing how it affected them; seeing the mental and physical damage it caused; my heart ached for them and..."

He looked at me intently.

"...my heart ached for you."

He took a breath like he was going to say more but then, he abruptly opened his door, got out and walked away, toward the fields. I got out, shut his door and watched him, wondering what he wanted to share.

The following months were filled with my travels for Francisco Farms and rebuilding my house. On Saturdays, I helped Machi with Kalani and sometimes attended church social or ministry events. When Dennis' beard and hair got long, I trimmed them. We talked about Jesus, the Bible, church, family, marriage, and just about everything else. I started wanting to be close to him; I started hating when the sessions were over. Sometimes, as we were talking, Dennis seemed to have something on his mind that he couldn't share.

At church one Sunday, the pastor said he had an announcement and he called me to the front. I went down, with no clue what he wanted. He motioned for me to stand on his right. Dennis walked toward me, got down on one knee, opened a ring box and lifted it to me. The congregation gasped, my mouth flew open and my hands flew up to cover it.

"Jane," Dennis said, looking up at me, "I won't be surprised at all if you reject me. I thought maybe you wouldn't in front of all these people."

The congregation laughed.

"If you accept me, I give you my solemn oath, I plan to prosper you and not harm you[12]. I will meet all your needs[13] and give you the desires of your heart.[14] I will be devoted to you."

It was obvious that Dennis was struggling to remember what he wanted to say. The pastor was mouthing the words along with Dennis. I kneeled down in front of Dennis and put my hands over his. He smiled, looked me in the eyes, and relaxed. He was looking at me the way my father did.

"I am compassionate and gracious; slow to anger, abounding in love and faithfulness,[15]" Dennis continued but he was speaking only to me. "When trials come, we will endure them together and grow stronger together. We will follow Jesus, the Bible and, with the power of the Holy Spirit, build a life of joy and peace."

Dennis looked up at the pastor who nodded then he looked at me.

"Jane, will you marry me?" he murmured. He was trembling.

The hundreds of people in the sanctuary were absolutely still.

"I will," I murmured back, mimicking him, touching his face, as the congregation applauded.

A week later, Dennis asked me to go with him to meet the parole officer. There had to be a hearing to get permission to take Dennis off of the medicine. Dennis wanted to have the wedding after the hearing. Even when I told him the medicine didn't matter, he was insistent that he wanted me to have a proper wedding night.

Actually, our daily routine after the proposal didn't change and we guessed our routine wouldn't change that much after we were married, except maybe if we had our own children. It dawned on me that, if I did get pregnant, I would be about the same age as my mother, and, my child would have two parents who were quiet, settled, happy, successful, fun to be with and available. I vowed, though, that my child would have plenty of social interaction, and we would have two children, even if we had to adopt.

The day of the hearing finally arrived and Dennis was given permission to go off the medicine. We planned the wedding for six months later. The ceremony and reception was held in our home. Though we had a good time, it was a relief when everyone left.

My body, seeming to realize a completely new experience was moments away, started reacting. It was trembling slightly as though electricity was pulsing through me. As I was putting away perishables, I realized Dennis wasn't in the house. Taking a few steps to a sliding glass door, I could see he was on the deck. I walked to him, put my hand on his arm and looked up at him. He was weeping.

"I slapped you in the face that night," he said. "I slapped you twice, hard."

Walking in front of him, I put my arms around his neck.

"I poked your eye out," I reminded him. "I think we're even."

He engulfed me with his strong arms as sobs of remorse escaped from the depths of his soul.

"I never knew I could feel like this," he finally stated.

"Same for me," I agreed.

Resting in his arms, I reminded him that I had a gift for him. He brushed his lips on mine and, this time, I didn't turn away. Instead, I brushed my lips on his.

We were joined together that night as the Bible said,[16] and I wouldn't have it any other way. I understood totally now why Machi wanted to be upstairs when Dean was showering. I understood why my mother worked to look good and attract her husband.

We had two children and 'used the money for good' as Ronald had requested by ministering to rapists and their victims. When Brad moved out of the cabin, we built additional cabins and started a church camp. We were living testimony that, as Jill said, "God is real".

---

[1] Revelation 19:7 KJV "Let us be glad and rejoice, and give honour to him (Jesus): for the marriage of the Lamb is come, and his wife (the Church) hath made herself ready."

[2] Matthew 19:6 KJV

[3] All terrain vehicle.

[4] All terrain vehicle

[5] Acts 19:2 KJV "He (Paul) said unto them (the disciples in Ephesus), Have ye received the Holy Ghost (Spirit) since ye believed? And they said unto him, We have not so much as heard whether there be any Holy Ghost (Spirit)."

[6] Genesis 2

[7] John 3:5 KJV "Except a man be born of water and of the Spirit, he cannot enter into the kingdom of God."

[8] John 16:13 KJV "Howbeit when he, the Spirit of truth, is come, he will guide you into all truth:"

[9] Hebrews 4

[10] Genesis 2:24 KJV "Therefore shall a man leave his father and his mother, and shall cleave unto his wife: and they shall be one flesh."

[11] Psalm 51:5 KJV "Behold, I was shapen in iniquity; and in sin did my mother conceive me."

[12] Jeremiah 29:11 KJV "For I know the thoughts that I think toward you, saith the Lord, thoughts of peace, and not of evil, to give you an expected end."

[13] Philippians 4:19 KJV "But my God shall supply all your need according to his riches in glory by Christ Jesus."

[14] Psalm 37:4 KJV "Delight thyself also in the Lord: and he shall give thee the desires of thine heart."

[15] Exodus 34:6 KJV "And the Lord passed by before him, and proclaimed, The Lord, The Lord God, merciful and gracious, longsuffering, and abundant in goodness and truth,"

[16] 1 Corinthians 6:16 KJV - "...for two...shall be one flesh."

Milton Keynes UK
Ingram Content Group UK Ltd.
UKHW010712080823
426520UK00001B/67